RIO REPRISAL

Life had taken on a new meaning for Jordan and all he wanted was to be left alone, but it was not to be. Back home, there were only blackened ruins and Mandy had been taken by the feared Apache, Wolf Taker. The only men Jordan could turn to for help were the outlaws with whom he had once ridden, but their price was high and bloody. Nevertheless, Jordan was prepared to tear the entire southwest apart as long as he found Mandy.

JAKE DOUGLAS

RIO REPRISAL

Complete and Unabridged

LINFORD
Leicester

First published in Great Britain in 1997 by
Robert Hale Limited
London

First Linford Edition
published 1999
by arrangement with
Robert Hale Limited
London

British Library CIP Data

Douglas, Jake
    Rio reprisal. — Large print ed.—
Linford western library
    1. Western stories
    2. Large type books
    I. Title
    823.9′14 [F]

ISBN 0–7089–5415–4

Published by
F. A. Thorpe (Publishing) Ltd.
Anstey, Leicestershire

Set by Words & Graphics Ltd.
Anstey, Leicestershire
Printed and bound in Great Britain by
T. J. International Ltd., Padstow, Cornwall

This book is printed on acid-free paper

For
another 'Whitehead'
— David
one of the good guys

1

West of the Wichita

The townsfolk of Diamondback Creek called Chris Jordan the quietest man west of the Wichita.

That's why they were so stunned when he was involved in some of the most savage violence ever seen in the town since the days of the brutal raids of Old Red Sleeves and his band of bloody Apaches.

It was a blue spring day, everything sharpcut and clean because of recent rain, a cooling breeze finding its way between the adobe buildings of the town only ten miles from the Texas State Line. Folk were out and about, chatting amicably, laughing, for it was that kind of day: it made everybody's heart sing. Jordan himself whistled an old Dixie tune quietly as

1

he shoulder-racked sacks of grain across the loading platform and dropped them into the back of his buckboard. He was sweating, but not excessively, and it felt good to give his muscles a work-out: he had told Talman, the storekeeper, he would do the loading himself and so expected a cent per bag discount, not tying-up a store employee to help.

Talman, middle-aged, greying at the temples and tending to wheeze — he was one of the few folk in town who didn't care much for spring because of the hayfever it brought him annually — smiled crookedly at the tall rancher.

'You'll have that herd in no time, Frank, you keep doin' business this way.'

Jordan smiled faintly, the movement softening the somewhat hard planes of his narrow, hawklike face. The leather-tanned skin around his pale-blue eyes crinkled.

'Ain't the herd I'm so worried about — it's the wedding.'

Talman whistled softly. 'So you finally

popped the question! And she must've said 'yes'!'

Jordan nodded, the smile widening slightly. 'She did.' He took the congratulatory hand that the storekeeper thrust at him and they shook briefly.

'Well, Mandy Prendergast has had plenty of offers over the years. Folk hereabouts were figurin' she might never get married. Too fussy, they figured — looks like she was just waitin' for the right man to come along.'

Talman frowned a little as he saw Jordan's smile stiffen about the edges and something came down behind those blue eyes . . . but only briefly. Then Jordan was smiling again, muscling another bag onto his wide shoulders and marching back across the platform towards his buckboard.

He whistled a few bars of the old Dixie tune and Talman, who had turned back to his desk, checking the lading bills in front of him, looked up curiously as the whistling suddenly stopped and a strange voice said sharply, 'Watch it with that sack, damn you!'

Jordan was lurching sideways, fighting to keep his balance, the sack slipping a little, two men looking at him hostilely. Talman had seen them earlier. They had come into his store and bought chewing tobacco and two cartons of .44 calibre shells, as well as beans and bacon and coffee. Men obviously intending to take to the trail, but, before leaving, figured to have a few drinks at the saloon first, according to the conversation he had heard.

That had been over an hour ago. Looked like they were headed back to the livery for their horses, still carrying their sacks of purchases.

And seemed they had come up on Jordan's blind side and he had cannoned into at least one of them with the sack. The dark-eyed man with the four-day shag of beard was the one who had spoken and who scowled now as Jordan turned slowly towards the men, already starting to apologize.

'Sorry, gents. Didn't see . . . '

Later, Talman wasn't sure if Jordan cut off the rest of his apology, or whether it was the second man, lank-haired and with a drooping moustache, who cut in abruptly and drowned out whatever Jordan had been about to say.

The moustached man sucked in a sharp breath through stained, tombstone teeth and said hoarsely, 'Judas priest, Tag! Look who we got here!'

The dark-eyed man frowned deeply as Jordan swung full-face towards them, his lips still parted, words frozen somewhere back in his throat as he stared at the men.

It was obvious to Talman that all three recognized each other.

But he wasn't prepared for the dark-eyed man's announcement: 'Jordan, you son of a bitch! We been lookin' for you for two years!'

The one with the moustaches had changed his sack from right hand to left now and flexed his fingers against the base of his gun holster.

Jordan wasn't wearing a gun. Never had since his arrival in town. In fact, what stunned Talman was that he knew the man as 'Frank Christian' — yet it was clear that the name 'Jordan' rocked him to his heels. His mouth closed and he flicked his blue eyes quickly from one man to the other, snapped his gaze towards Talman, but looked away swiftly. He heaved the sack of grain off his shoulder and it struck the corner of the buck-board's tailgate, ripping and spilling a golden cascade before thudding to the ground. He ignored it, facing the two men who both had their hands close to their holstered sixguns now.

'What lousy twist of luck set you two crossing my trail?' he said quietly, eyes narrowing, Talman shocked by the change that came over the man.

This loner, he knew as Frank Christian — as all the town knew him — had always been taciturn, quietly polite, sober-faced, but pleasant to most everyone. The storekeeper had never seen his face take on the chipped-granite look that showed right now, never seen those pleasant blue eyes slit down to chips of snowline stream-ice, never seen that wide, slow-smiling mouth compress into the razor slash it had now become.

And he had sure never seen the big hands curl into hard-knuckled fists the way they were doing now.

'So it is you then!' breathed the moustached one. 'Just for a moment I figured mebbe I'd made a mistake. You look different without that frontier moustache and the long hair.'

'I thought you were dead long since, Ollie,' Jordan replied, swivelling his stare to the other man. 'And I heard you had to run to Mexico, Tag . . . with some young gal's kin hard on your tail.'

'You forget what you heard about us,' Tag growled. 'We're here now, and so're you. Let's go someplace we can talk private.'

He reached out with his left hand to grab Jordan's arm. The man stepped back and to one side, slamming a hammerblow on to the inside of Tag's arm. The force swung the arm way out from the bearded man's body, causing him to stumble.

'No,' Jordan said flatly and Talman felt his own jaw sag as he watched Ollie slap leather and get a gun out in mighty slick time, only to have it smashed from his hand by Jordan's down-striking fist. The sixgun thudded to the planks of the loading platform and by then Tag, cursing, shaking his numbed right arm, moved in swinging his left fist. Talman started to call a warning but Jordan was already crouched, turning at the same time, piling a fist into the man's midriff. Tag gasped and stumbled, legs buckling.

Jordan swung back, straightening in time to meet Ollie's rush. He parried the first blow, lifting his arm upwards and taking Ollie's arm with it. It left the lean body unprotected and Jordan hit the man in the ribs, shouldered him back against the store wall, and rammed his head up under Ollie's jaw while he pummelled his mid-section with blurring fists. Ollie gagged and would have fallen except that Jordan's pressure held him there.

Then Tag came lurching in, bringing up a knee into Jordan's side, knocking the man halfway across the platform. He went down, skidding, and Tag leapt at him, thrusting both boots out in front of him. Jordan rolled clear off the raised platform and before Tag had recovered from his jarring landing, grabbed one of the man's legs and heaved. Tag hit hard, the back of his head cracking audibly. Talman was surprised to see Jordan, instead of running clear as he might have expected him to do, leap up on to the platform, and come charging at both men. Tag was rolling aside, dazed, but Jordan lashed a boot against his ribs, stepped on the man's belly, on his way to meet the snarling Ollie.

The moustached man held a wicked-looking knife now, teeth bared as he came in crouching, slashing. Jordan's features sharpened as he leapt back. Ollie laughed once, slashed again and the tip of the blade ripped Jordan's sleeve, drew a red streak of blood. It was the only chance he had and he'd botched it.

Jordan grabbed the knife hand, somehow twisted it up under his armpit and savagely bent the wrist until Talman heard the bones snap and he felt sick as Ollie collapsed, moaning.

Jordan kicked Tag in the middle of the face as the man was getting up, hurling him back flailing against the wall. A crowed had gathered now and men were yelling as Jordan went after Tag but the bearded man lifted a boot abruptly and it caught Jordan in the middle of the chest. He went back fast, heel catching on an uneven board, going down hard. His head struck his buckboard and he saw an explosion of fireworks behind his eyes.

Then Talman was yelling, 'Frank! He's got a gun!'

Through the red haze in front of his

eyes, Jordan looked towards Tag. I
was Ollie who had the gun, snatc
up his fallen Peacemaker in his left
hand, sobbing with the pain of his
broken wrist. He fired and Jordan felt
the burn of the slug across the tip of his
right shoulder as he rolled away. The
crowed scattered as Tag palmed up his
own gun and shot at the moving Jordan.
Splinters erupted in several places
around Jordan's body and then Talman
bawled, '*Here!*'

Jordan saw the rifle turning end for
end as the storekeeper hurled it towards
him, having snatched it from its peg
where it normally rested above the small
desk.

He reacted instinctively; he spun,
snatching the rifle out of the air,
dropping to one knee, with the lever
closing and his finger on the trigger
already.

There was a roar of gunfire as he
worked lever and trigger in a blur and
Ollie lifted to his toes, jerked as two
more slugs punched into his mean, lean

body and then fell sprawling across Talman's desk. Tag got off one more shot that dusted the brim of Jordan's hat and then the bearded man showed sheer terror on his face as he cried 'No!' and started to spin away.

He was cut down in a fresh hail of bullets, dead before his body hit the boards, blood soaking into the weathered wood.

A deathly silence suddenly gripped the town; almost as if every living thing in Diamondback Creek ceased to breathe for a few seconds. Even the pariah dogs and roosters in private chicken pens were quiet.

Then it was broken by a big, heavy boot crunching on to the leading platform and a deep voice saying, 'I'll take the rifle, Frank.'

Jordan blinked through the stinging gunsmoke and saw the bulky man standing there, one hand resting on the butt of his sixgun, the other outstretched to take the smoking rifle. The spring sunlight glinted off the tin star pinned to the worn serge vest the man wore over a creased white shirt with frayed collar and cuffs.

Sheriff Andy Plumm, a hard though generally fair man, and one who was short on patience.

So Jordan lowered the gun hammer, reversed the rifle and slapped the butt into the lawman's big hand.

'It was self-defence, Sheriff,' Jordan said, in a voice he might have wished was some steadier than it sounded to him.

'Started out that way, all right,' Plumm allowed. 'I saw that much. But you had both men dead on their feet and you still kept pumping lead into 'em. Let's go to my office, Frank.'

'They started it, Andy,' Talman said, stepping forward. 'They were gonna kill Frank. And you know he don't carry a gun.'

Plumm's hard eyes sought Jordan's face. 'He sure knows how to use one, though.'

★ ★ ★

Two hours later, Jordan was still in the law office with Plumm and Deputy Arch Greenwood standing with his shoulder against the door frame, holding a carbine kind of casually, but with the hammer spur ready beneath his thumb.

Jordan couldn't keep his exasperation in check any longer. 'C'mon, Andy! I've work to do back at the ranch. What the hell else can I tell you? You've been and taken statements. It was clearly selfdefence . . . '

'That ain't what's botherin' me,' the sheriff cut in, pursing his lips as he held Jordan's gaze. 'Both Talman and that man of his, Pierce, or whatever his name is . . . '

'Pearson,' said Arch Greenwood. 'Donnie Pearson, Sher'ff.'

Plumm ignored the deputy. 'Both of 'em heard those two dead men call you 'Jordan' — and you never denied it. You seemed to know 'em.'

14

Jordan sighed. 'I told you. Tag W and Ollie Braun: hardcases I knew ⌐ trail drive years ago. I crossed 'em because I was trail boss and they brought booze into the camp and I kicked their butts outa there. It was in Injun country, north of the Red River, and they nearly lost their scalps. They swore they'd square with me. This is the first time we've crossed trails since.'

Plumm stared levelly, drumming thick fingers on his desk. 'Frank, you've never caused no trouble since you come here six months ago. You're polite; you don't smile or talk a lot, but you pay your bills, owe no man, and generally get along with folk — now why is it that I got me such an odd feelin' about your story and these two hardcases you nailed? Think it could be because no one's ever even seen you with a gun, then when them two made their try for you, you sent 'em to glory as fast and deadly as anyone I've ever seen — on either side of the law. I gotta wonder about that, Frank. And that means I gotta wonder about any story you tell me.'

Jordan suddenly stood up and Greenwood straightened, carbine cocked now. Plumm watched warily.

'Andy, I've told you how it was. You don't believe me, then you set about proving I'm a liar. But do it on your time . . . I've got chores to get done.'

He turned and strode right up to the deputy.

'You gonna move, Arch?'

Greenwood looked past the tall man's shoulder and, after a slight hesitation, Plumm nodded.

'Just don't leave the district, Frank,' the sheriff called after Jordan as he made for the street door.

Jordan didn't answer, made his way past the small throng that had gathered outside the law office, crossed over to the store side, then turned down the alley to the loading platform. Talman had had Pearson finish the loading and the buckboard was parked in the shade of a tree beyond the store, the team

16

hobbled on a nearby patch of grass. Jordan waved his thanks to Talman as he made his way across and started to put the team back into harness.

He heard footsteps behind him as he backed the lead horse between the shafts and thought it was Talman so didn't look around. Until a voice said, 'Frank, I rode in as soon as I heard! Are you all right?'

He spun around, swallowing a curse as he saw Mandy Prendergast in riding gear coming quickly towards him, her golden hair spilling to her shoulders from beneath the small hat. He took her into his arms and hugged her to him, wincing a little as her own hug put pressure on his aching ribs.

'Oh, I was so worried!' the girl said into his shoulder. 'I — I couldn't believe it! Not about you, Frank! Not mixed up in a gunfight!'

By then Mandy was stepping back, looking up into his bruised and cut face. He forced a smile.

'Couldn't believe it myself. Hadn't

seen those hardcases in years,' he told her, feeling the wrench at his belly as the lie came so easily to his lips. And was followed by others as he told her the same story about Tag and Ollie as he had told Sheriff Plumm.

Her grey eyes flicked over his face after his explanation. He thought he saw doubt on her lovely face 'Someone said you handled that rifle like a — a gunfighter.'

He smiled, shrugging. 'You learn to shoot straight and fast on trail drives through Indian country, Mandy. I told you, too, I'd fought in the war.'

She nodded, grooving lines showing between her eyes. 'Ye-es, you did, Frank, but, I've just realized, I — I hardly know anything about you!'

He laughed shortly, grabbing her by the arms and pulling her close to him. 'Just think what fun you'll have finding out after we're married!'

She started to laugh but he kissed her, stifling it. The kiss didn't last for long. A harsh voice broke them apart.

'I don't think Mandy will be finding out any more about you than she knows already, Frank. There isn't going to be any wedding.'

Jordan felt the girl stiffen and a shaft of coldness shot through his belly as he looked over Mandy's golden head to the stern face of Miles Prendergast, her father.

The rancher was backed up by his foreman and several gun-hung cowboys.

'Dad, what — what d'you mean?' Mandy gasped.

'I said it plain enough, girl. I've always suspected there was something in this man's past he wasn't telling us. It seems he hasn't even told us his real name. Now don't you concern yourself with this, Daughter. You ride on back to the ranch with Cliff and Al. Frank — or whoever he is — and I will have us a little talk and lay our cards on the table. All of them.'

She opened her mouth to protest but her father held up a hand quickly and she said nothing. She didn't even struggle as two cowboys came forward, took an arm each and led her away.

Jordan set his brittle gaze on Miles Prendergast.

'Damn you, Miles! You've about broken her spirit with your demanding ways!'

'That's no concern of yours, drifter . . . not any longer.'

'I still aim to marry her.'

Prendergast shook his head slowly. 'No. You'll be taken back to your ranch and allowed to pack your gear. Then you'll be escorted to the state line. And if ever you try to see Mandy again, you'll be shot on sight. Do I make myself clear?'

Jordan said nothing. There didn't seem to be a hell of a lot he *could* say. Not with four cocked guns pointing at him, held in the hands of hardeyed *hombres* who would shoot him where he stood if Prendergast gave the order.

'Let's go, Frank,' the rancher said coldly, lighting a cheroot. 'The sooner there are a lot of miles between you and my daughter, the better I'll feel.'

'How about Mandy's feelings?'

'She has no say in this. She's not yet reached her majority, and won't for another eleven months. By that time, she'll have forgotten she ever knew you; I'll make damn sure of that!'

Jordan knew that was true. Prendergast was a hard-bitten man of the old school, straight-laced, strict, a church-every-Sunday type — and he ruled his ranch and family with an iron fist. No doubt he would square-away Sheriff Plumm and Plumm would go along with whatever Prendergast did.

Well, maybe it was best. The thought slammed into his brain like a fist jarring against his jaw. Hell, the past had come back to haunt him — as he had always known it would. Sometime.

And that sometime had arrived.

It would be best for everyone, including Mandy — maybe *especially* Mandy — if he just cleared out. Plumm wouldn't let it go now. He'd investigate until he came up with something to explain away why Tag had called him 'Jordan'.

Then that really would end things and Mandy would be devastated. Not that she wouldn't be hurt and shaken now if he went along with her father and these men and rode out of her life forever. But . . .

He raised bleak eyes to Prendergast and the man took an involuntary step backward, startled by the coldness of the stare.

'All right, Prendergast, let's go. You won't need those men.'

'I maybe won't *need* them, but I'm bringing them along just the same.'

Jordan smiled crookedly as he turned back to the buckboard. Just like Miles Prendergast: the man had to have the last word.

2

Border Country

Jordan wasn't a man given to hard drinking but he wished right now that he had a bottle of redeye within reach. He figured he could drain it without taking the neck away from his lips.

He sat back from the small campfire on a rounded rock, smoking, cupping the cigarette in his hand — old habits die hard, he thought with a grim smile. Abruptly, he kicked the edge of the fire, scattering the coals, leaving only a small cone in the centre that would slowly burn down during the night. He stood, pressing hands into the small of his back, rolling his head to ease the stiffness in the back of his neck. Looking up at the stars, he stayed that way for a few minutes, trying to make his mind a blank but unsuccessfully.

Hell, it would be a long, long time before he could blank out the memory of Mandy Prendergast — and the happenings of this day that was fast dying. He glanced once more at the waning moon and figured it must be close to midnight and he wasn't doing a damn thing for himself or anyone else sitting here moping.

He rigged the bedroll with his saddle-bags and spare clothes, leaving his hat on the end against his saddle so that it looked like he was sleeping there. Then he moved back into the rocks with a spare blanket and spread it on the pine branches he had prepared earlier while appearing to look for firewood. Yeah, old habits died hard, all right.

These past months he had grown used to sleeping with a roof over his head, even if it was the crude sod-and-shingle affair on the log cabin he had built for Mandy. He swore softly. There she was again: intruding into his thoughts. Well, he knew she'd be there for a long time yet. He'd never been in love before and he wasn't quite prepared for the wrenching hell his departure from Diamondback Creek promised to bring. Mandy was the only reason he'd gone quietly. Hell, she could do a heap better than him: he was honest enough to admit that to himself. Way, way better. If she'd known the truth about him, he would never have even got to first base — Miles would have seen to that!

'All *right*!' he hissed aloud. 'It's finished now! Leave it be!'

Of course it wouldn't let him be, and he tossed and turned on the pine branches, blaming the unfamiliar feel of the guns he kept with him. It had been a long time since he had slept with his rifle and sixgun. He'd had to clean and oil both weapons, they had been out of use for so long.

He smiled ruefully, lying on his back now, staring once more up at the stars. It might be a spell since he had toted firearms, but he sure hadn't forgotten how to use them.

Just ask Tag and Ollie.

He smiled bitterly. *Goddamn* the luck that had brought those two to Diamondback Creek! If they had skirted the town instead of . . .

He stiffened suddenly.

Someone was out there, moving in stealthily on his camp. Not an Indian, even though this was Indian country. He would never have heard an Apache coming in: the first he would have known would be the knife blade slicing across his throat.

No, this was someone else, a white man, pretty damn good at creeping around a man's night camp, but not quite good enough.

He rolled off the edge of the green pine boughs and slowly and silently worked the newly oiled Winchester's lever. He lowered the hammer under his thumb, rammed his sixgun into his belt and, in stockinged feet, made his way towards the dull glow of the campfire's coals and the decoy bedroll.

Just in time to see a dark shape

hunched over the made-up bedroll, reach out towards the hat.

He stood up, deliberately cocking the hammer loudly. The figure spun towards him fast, too fast: the shadowy shape sprawled awkwardly.

'Stay just like that!' Jordan snapped. 'One move and I'll put a bullet through you.'

He heard a sharp sucking-in of breath, then: 'Don't shoot, Frank! It's me! Mandy!'

His senses reeled. The very last person he expected — or wanted — to see. He eased down the hammer, stepped forward, angling the Winchester towards the ground, out to one side.

'The hell're you doing here?' he demanded harshly, as she climbed to her feet and started to brush herself down.

She paused at his tone and turned her pale face towards him, the golden hair sheened with starlight now the small hat had fallen off.

'Well, I must say that's a hell of a way

to greet the woman who's cut all her family ties and ridden hard for eight long hours, just to be with you — for the rest of her life!'

It took a moment for her words to sink in and when they did, he dropped the rifle and opened his arms and she ran into them, crushing herself against him, crying and laughing all at the same time.

★ ★ ★

They were riding through harsh country in the pre-dawn light now, the girl dozing in the saddle of her sorrel. Jordan looked at her with fondness, but it was touched by a fear he had never known before . . . the fear that this was not the right thing to do. Mandy deserved someone much better than him: he had told her so on several occasions but she had only laughed and stopped his protests with a warm kiss. *That* made him forget his apprehension — for a time, leastways.

It was back at full power now as they rode. This was one hell of a woman, he thought. Not yet twenty-one, having endured years of obedience and subjugation from her father, then not only did she stand up to him and tell him she was going to marry Jordan no matter what, she then rode all that way through Apache country, tracked him down in the darkness . . .

Frowning, he turned to her as she stirred. 'Just how did you find me?'

She took a moment to comprehend and then smiled. 'Cliff Holdway — he's always had something of a shine for me. I . . . sort of worked on him a little and he told me where they had put you across the state line. I'd ridden through this country on the El Paso stage — I told you about it, if you remember?'

He nodded. 'Yeah, some maiden aunt wanted you for a companion when she was sick.' He smiled ruefully. 'And I happened to tell you then about the time a bunch of Mescaleros hunted down my pard and me when we were scouting a trail for a wagon train gathering in Sante Fe. By God, Mandy, you've a good memory to recollect that draw where we camped and the rocks that formed a kinda cave on the slope — and then to find it in the dark.'

She smiled. 'See? When you're in love, you can do anything.'

He smiled back but sobered quickly. 'Your father'll send someone or come after you.'

She surprised him by shaking her head. 'No.' There was sadness in her voice and on her face: it was light enough for him to make out her expression. 'No, he laid down the law for me: if I did this thing, went looking for you and married you, then I-I no longer had a family. I was no longer his daughter, and he never wanted to hear from me nor set eyes on me again . . . '

'Judas, Mandy!' Jordan's voice was barely audible. 'I can't let you do this! You can't cut yourself off from your family because of someone like me.'

She tossed her head, the golden hair

fanning briefly, and he caught the glint of tear tracks through the trail dust on her cheeks.

'I'm not doing it for someone *like* you, Frank — I'm doing it for *you*! No one else.'

He was silent for a long spell and as they were topping-out on a sawbacked ridge, he said quietly, 'My name's Chris Jordan, Mandy, not Frank Christian.' He waited but she said nothing and he continued quietly, 'I'm on the run. Not from the law — I've squared away with that. But there're a few men who'd like to get their hands on me. It doesn't matter why, but — those two back in Diamondback Creek were part of the bunch I'm talking about.'

She was looking steadily into his face now as he set his buckskin in close. 'They want to kill you?'

'They will kill me eventually, but first . . .'

'Fra — What do I call you? Chris?'

'That's my name. Christian Franklin Jordan.' He tried to make it sound light but that wasn't the kind of mood either of them were in right now.

'Chris — I'll get used to it.' She smiled briefly.

'Mandy, you better wait until I tell you the rest.'

She leaned from the saddle and pressed a finger against his lips. 'Hush. It's enough that you've told me what you have. Whatever it is happened long ago, before I knew you. It's past, gone forever. You were living an honest life and it's no fault of yours that you're here now. So, we can make a new start from this moment and forget all that's happened before — except, of course, the good parts!' Her smile flashed wider. 'We'll be married and start out as Mr and Mrs Chris Jordan.'

'I wasn't aiming on just abandoning that ranch your father dragged me away from, Mandy. I was gonna go back and — well, I was gonna go back.'

Her smile vanished. 'There's no need, Chris. I have a little money of my own. You were proving-up on that land. We can find another place and we'll work it together. We'll make a success of it, you'll see.'

Her youthful enthusiasm set his blood coursing wildly through his veins and he didn't speak for a time, thinking of what she had said. If only they could do it!

Well, why not? He'd never thought he could step into ranching the way he had after — well, after the other kind of life he'd led, but it had been working well enough until . . .

And there it was, that damn word: *until. If . . .*

It could happen again, accidentally like Tag and Ollie spotting him, or maybe Loomis turning up. He wasn't the kind to give up, and word would get back to him sooner or later about the fate of Tag and Ollie.

'We don't have to go in for ranching, you know,' she said suddenly, startling him. 'There are plenty of other businesses we can start.'

He turned to look at this marvellous

young woman beside him and he knew right then that it *would* work — whatever they chose to do together — it *would* . . . it *would* . . .

★   ★   ★

Miles Prendergast was walking along the street opposite the law office when he heard his name called. His face wore a perpetual scowl these days and his mouth tightened as he saw Sheriff Andy Plumm waving from the office stoop. The rancher kept on walking, ignoring the man's sign to come join him in the office.

Plumm swore softly to himself and then hurried across the street to intercept the rancher outside Harvey's Mercantile. Plumm was panting a little from the exertion, told himself for the thousandth time he must get more exercise: sprawling all day in his desk chair wasn't good enough for a man his age.

'Miles!' wheezed the sheriff, stepping

into the path of the bleak-eyed rancher. 'I've got some news.'

Prendergast stopped, his hard eyes staring hostilely. 'News about what?' he snapped.

'Your daughter and . . . '

'I have no daughter. Anything you have to say about the woman who once called herself my daughter holds no interest for me whatsoever. Now step aside, Plumm, I'm a busy man.'

The sheriff didn't move and Prendergast made an exasperated sound and stepped around him quickly, ramming him sharply with a shoulder. Plumm staggered, turned, looked at the retreating back.

'I think his name's Chris Jordan.'

Prendergast stopped, paused, then started forward again, without turning. But he was not walking so fast now.

'*Christian* Jordan — which is likely why he used the name of Frank Christian while he was here.' The rancher kept walking, the sheriff following several paces behind, folk turning to stare and listen. 'If he's the one, he did time in a Texas State Prison. For armed hold-up.'

Prendergast stopped now, turned slowly. 'He's an outlaw?'

'Strictly speakin', not any longer. He served his time for holdin' up a train near San Antone. The gang stole an express box. No one killed, but the money was never recovered. Jordan was wounded and left behind. That's how come he was picked up and tossed into jail.'

'Why're you telling me this, Plumm?'

The sheriff's patience was at an end. 'Because I thought you'd be interested, that's why! Whether you claim you no longer have a daughter or not, fact remains Mandy still *is* your flesh and blood, and that's the kind of man she's run off with.'

Prendergast looked pale now, his sunken eyes dark and menacing, lips compressed. He suddenly jerked his head. 'Well, you certainly took your time getting even that amount of information! It's months since this Jordan was kicked across the state line.'

'Took me some time to work my way through all the outlaws who could fit the bill,' complained the lawman, angry that he was receiving such a cold reception after all the work he had put in on this, thinking to curry favour with Prendergast. 'I ain't one to give up easy, Miles, damnit!'

'What's the point?' the rancher asked wearily. 'You've said Jordan is no longer wanted. Why bother?'

Plumm's face tightened. 'Yeah, good question!' he growled, turning away abruptly. Then he swung back, adding, 'But damned if I'd like any daughter of mine to run off and marry an ex-jail-bird!'

Angrily he strode back across the street and Prendergast called to him just as he reached the far side. 'You didn't say where he is now!'

Plumm turned slowly, smiling tautly. 'Because I dunno — and, after the last few minutes, I no longer care, Miles! Good-day to you!'

The lawman slammed his office door behind him and folk stared at Miles Prendergast where he still stood in the middle of the boardwalk. Then he glared at them and shook the quirt strapped to his left wrist.

'Get on with your business! And mind your own affairs!'

'Mebbe you oughta take your own advice, Prendergast!' a man's voice called from the ranks of the crowd as they dispersed and Miles snapped, 'Who said that? By Godfrey, no one in this jerk-water town sasses me that way and gets away with it!'

But the folk dispersed and he stood there trembling with rage and frustration, realizing he would never know who had spoken out.

Thing was, the man, whoever he had been, had spoken the truth: despite everything and the way he felt about Mandy, maybe he ought to do something about this information he had just been given.

Maybe.

But Miles Prendergast was stubborn and didn't give ground easy.

He stormed on down the walk, head down, shoulders hunched, and folk gave way before him like grass stalks parting ahead of a powerful wind.

★　★　★

The Indian was already drunk, likely on the local brew of *tiswin*, and when he demanded a brassbound oaken beaker of rum in exchange for his fine buffalo robe, Jordan shook his head adamantly.

'No rum, Wolf Taker.' He crossed his hands and spread them outwards in the sign of refusal. 'Washington-Man forbids it, you know that.'

Wolf Taker was big for an Apache, especially a Chiracahua, big and not unhandsome, despite the wolf-jaw scars on the left side of his face. His muscles rippled down his body: he wore only the wild Apache's breechclout and the long thigh-length moccasins rolled down to his knees. He clutched a well-used '66

Winchester rifle, the stock repaired with a rawhide sleeve and studded with brass tacks in the Indian way. He wore a knife in a fringed leather sheath on his left hip and — unusual for an Indian — a sixgun was rammed into the rawhide strip that held up his breechclout.

His dark eyes glittered as they looked at Jordan leaning his arms on the counter-edge now and there was hate on his face. Jordan wasn't unduly perturbed. Wolf Taker hated all white-eyes, men, women or children — it was well-known. He despised everything white, yet he craved the white-man's whiskey and rum, his warm blankets and iron knives and bullets . . . and Wolf Taker was intelligent enough to despise himself for this same craving.

Yet he turned up here at the isolated border country trading post with buffalo hides and mountain lion skins, even a few beaver skins, wanting to trade for white-man goods that he could never get on the reservation.

Mostly he and his companions were

here illegally, away from the reservation without permission, but Jordan never called the army as he was supposed to do or notified the Indian agents who would make life hell for the Apaches when they were returned.

Jordan had always been free — except for those years in the Texas prison — and he sympathized with the Indians being restricted to reservations. They were a nomadic, hunter-gatherer people, and he could well imagine the hell they must go through depending on the white man for every mouthful of food. With some of the agents they never did get their rightful ration and many slowly starved.

Hell, he wouldn't blame any man for bustingout under those circumstances. What kind of man could sit idly by and watch his family starve or freeze? No, to hell with regulations that said he *must* report any Indians who could not produce written cards giving them permission to be off the reservation.

It had earned him a couple of sharp

reprimands from the army and once he had gotten into a brutal knock-down, drag-out fight with a corrupt Indian agent, but he didn't change.

The Indians probably didn't like him any better than any other white man but they did show him a little more respect. Not that he was looking for it or anything else. This was just the way he was built and he aimed to stay that way.

Now he met Wolf Taker's sullen gaze and said, 'What'll it be, Wolf? Three knives? Twenty-five rounds of ammo for your rifle? How about a one gallon iron kettle? Or a yard and a half of calico for your woman? I can give you three dozen iron arrowheads?'

The Apache swayed, his eyes dulled with *tiswin* and simmering hatred. 'I take bullets!'

'OK,' Jordan turned back to his shelves, took down two cartons of .44 calibre cartridges, slid one across to Wolf Taker and counted out five from the other box. He added an extra five, spilled them into the Indian's big hand.

'I'll give you thirty — that was a winter robe you brought in. And I'm not asking how you came by it at this time of year.' Likely the man had fought its original owner or cheated him at dice or some other gambling game they used to while away the long dreary reservation hours.

The Apache put the rifle cartridges into his rawhide pouch inside his breechclout, hefted the Winchester and glared at Jordan across the counter.

'I take bullets, but maybe I give them back to you sometime . . . .' He lifted a stiffened forefinger and flicked his thumb like a falling gun hammer, baring strong white teeth in a humourless smile before turning and striding out of the dimness of the trading post.

When the door clattered close behind him, Mandy came out from behind the curtain which separated the living-quarters from the business section of the store. She looked older than her twenty-two years, more weathered, but she was still mighty handsome and her figure curved the faded calico dress tantalizingly.

'I'm glad he's gone. Chris, he's one Indian I wish you'd report to the army or the agents. He . . . frightens me.'

Jordan smiled and slid an arm about her slim waist. 'He don't mean anything personal, Mandy. He just don't like whites and I can't find it in myself to blame him.'

'But he looks so angry when he's been drinking! The way he looks at me — I-I feel like he's stripping me of my clothes.'

'Well, I might kinda draw the line at that, I guess,' Jordan said lazily. 'I'm the only one allowed to do that — least-ways, I hope I am.'

'Oh, you!' Mandy punched him none too lightly on the shoulder and then she smiled, moved closer and toyed with the front of his shirt. 'It's not likely we'll have any more customers today is it? Why don't we close early and . . . well, I need a bath anyway and you could scrub my back.'

He laughed, was already on his way around the corner to drop the bar in place across the door.

'Oh-oh,' he said, stopping Mandy in her tracks as she headed towards the curtain. 'Better postpone that bath, we got visitors.'

'Oh! Who is it?' She sounded mildly annoyed and he winked.

'John Banton and some of his men, looks like. Cornell, too.'

Mandy frowned. 'But they're all ranchers. They buy their goods in town, not from us — except once in a while when they run short . . . '

The men had dismounted now and stomped across the porch. Jordan opened the door for them and shook hands with Johnny Banton, a prosperous young rancher from up the valley. His foreman and two cowhands filed in after him, followed by Ric Cornell, another rancher but older, and Banton's neighbour.

All the men removed their hats when they saw Mandy and greeted her warmly. She smiled at them all and said she had coffee warming and had just finished baking biscuits.

They sat down at the few rickety tables around the unlit potbelly stove almost before she had finished speaking. Mandy's cooking was held in high regard right throughout the valley and beyond.

When they each held a mug of steaming coffee and were putting away as many hot biscuits as they decently could, Banton looked levelly at Jordan and said, 'Seen that Wolf Taker ridin' out as we came down valley.'

'Doing a little trading,' Jordan replied easily.

'Heard he half killed a 'breed buffalo hunter in Kincaid in a fight over cards,' Cornell put in in his heavy voice. 'They say he took his robes in payment for what the 'breed owed him.'

Cornell was looking pointedly at the piled buffalo robe draped carelessly on one end of the counter.

'That so?' Jordan said, and that was

all he said by way of reply.

'That damn Injun needs takin' down a peg or two,' Cornell growled. 'Altogether too blamed arrogant for my likin'.'

'And the likin' of most other whites,' growled Banton, but added quickly before anyone could take up the conversation. 'But we come to talk about beeves, not buffalo.'

Jordan looked puzzled.

'Three nights from now,' Cornell said quietly, 'it's gonna be what we call an Apache moon round these here parts. Oh, don't look alarmed, Miz Franklin,' the rancher spoke swiftly when he saw Mandy's face. 'It don't mean nothin' these days. Years ago, it meant Apaches might pull a raid on the settlers because the moon was dark, see? Right along the border, down south of Banton's there, they call it a rustler's moon because it's good and dark for drivin' stolen cows across the Rio.'

'And three nights from now,' Mandy said slowly, looking from her husband to

Cornell and Banton, 'we're going to have a night when the moon is dark . . . is that right?'

Cornell nodded, looking somewhat uneasy now. He scowled at Banton and nodded for him to carry on.

'Mandy, you must've heard talk about these border spreads often stocking up by takin' a short run across the Rio and cuttin' out a few dozen head from one of the big Mexican *ranchos* down there. They got thousands of acres of land they never even seen, can't begin to have any kinda accurate tally of the number of cows they run.'

'I understand what you're saying, John,' she told him soberly. 'But that doesn't make it right for anyone from north of the Rio to go down and just . . . take them. It's stealing however you look at it. Rustling if you like.'

'Now easy, Mandy,' Jordan snapped. 'You don't even hint that a man's a rustler without getting yourself in a heap of trouble down in this neck of the woods.'

Banton laughed. 'Relax, Chris, I ain't offended and neither are the others. OK, we admit to throwin' a wide loop over that Mex stock now and again. Everyone along the border does it, horses, cows . . . they're all unbranded and runnin' wild. The *ranchero* doesn't even miss 'em. And don't think they came by 'em so honest in the first place. I can remember my grandpappy tellin' about the fights between his cowboys and the Mex *vaqueros* who raided up from below the Rio to cut out good Texas steers and mustangs.'

Mandy started to speak but Jordan caught her eye and shook his head, spoke before she could decide what she was going to do. 'What does this have to do with me, Johnny?'

Banton, a man with a youthful face although he was in his mid-thirties, about the same age as Jordan, smiled widely. 'Chris, we know the tradin'-post business ain't going as well as it was when you first took over from ol'

49

Fadeaway Farrell, but you been OK to us ranchers, lettin' us have stores on the slate when we got caught short and so on.' He leaned across the table. 'We've had word that old Nan Tan Lupan himself, General Crook, has ordered out a lot more army patrols to put down the Apaches once and for all. He needs beef, more than he can lay his hands on in Arizona, and the government's payin' top dollar — ' He waved a hand around at Cornell and the others.

'So we figured to make a little sortie down south of the Rio three nights from now, pick us up a few hundred head and run 'em back up here, then sell 'em to the army — for a nice profit. You could earn yourself five hundred bucks or more if you ride with us and help on the drive. I know you done trail-drivin' in the past . . . you interested?'

Jordan flicked his gaze to Mandy, saw her frowning in consternation, but he swung back to Banton and nodded slowly. 'I'd be interested.'

'Chris!' Mandy said sharply. 'I feel strongly about this — it's just out-and-out rustling.' She looked at the tight-faced Cornell and the others defiantly. 'I don't care if you're offended or not, you're riding down into Mexico to steal another man's cattle. You can rationalize all you like, but that's what you're doing and I for one want no part of it.'

She turned and stormed back through the curtain and the store was quiet for a spell and then Johnny Banton sighed, looked at Jordan and spread his hands palms upward.

'Sorry, *amigo*, didn't mean to start any trouble. Just figured you could use the *dinero* . . . but we'll be movin' on and . . . '

Jordan didn't move as the others stood and Banton called out his thanks for the coffee and biscuits to the unseen Mandy. She didn't reply.

'What time you leaving for the Rio?' asked Jordan quietly.

The others looked at him sharply and then Cornell spoke in that heavy, deep voice of his. 'Sat'dee at sundown. We aim to be at the Rio by moonset and then we got till sun-up to gather what we want and get 'em back across the river.'

He was watching Jordan closely as he spoke and Banton added, 'We don't think there'll be any *vaqueros* to worry about but you never know — might be a little lead-tradin'. Sure to be some hard ridin'.'

Jordan smiled. 'Pick me up here on your way through.'

'Sure?' Banton asked.

Now Jordan stood, glancing towards the curtain. He nodded. 'I'm sure.'

'We'll see you then, Chris. Bring your guns.'

He looked pointedly at Jordan's waist: he hadn't worn his sixgun since buying and opening this old trading post called Fadeaway's Fare.

'I'll bring 'em,' Jordan promised, saw the riders off into the late afternoon and then barred the door from inside and walked slowly towards the curtain — and Mandy waiting beyond.

'You're going,' she said as he pushed the curtain aside. 'No, I didn't hear, but I know you by now, Chris.'

He walked right up to her and she didn't move, merely tilted her head so she could look up into his face. He placed his hands gently on her shoulders.

'Mandy, I know you're not happy here at the trading post. I've been selfish, I guess. I figured staying out here away from everyone, there'd be less chance of someone coming by and recognizing me. But I hadn't given any thought to you. You ain't used to this kind of lonely life, not seeing other women except the occasional squaw or, once in a while, the women from ranches up the valley. It's been bothering me for quite a spell. But, if I ride with Banton and Cornell and make five hundred bucks or more — in *one night*! Well, we can sell and with that extra cash move on and buy ourselves a small ranch closer to some town that'll give you a little social life . . . '

She was crying and hugging him before he was finished.

3

Apache Moon

It was dark when the Texan cavalcade splashed their mounts across the shallow Rio ford.

The moon had set earlier, what there was of it, and the stars were not yet bright enough to see much by. There were more than a dozen riders making the crossing, and already two or three sat their mounts with rifle butts resting on their thighs, bullets in chambers, ready for anything.

The border patrols, both Mexican and American, were far to the west along the river at this time.

The men had removed their spurs and metal bits, replacing them with greenhide bridles in the Indian fashion. The horses' hoofs would be muffled with pads of burlap or rawhide once they were closer to the country where the *rancho*'s cattle were allowed to run free.

Jordan had his rifle resting across his thighs as his buckskin heaved up out of the river and on to the sandy bank where the others were gathering.

'We go a mile and a half south then make a sharp turn west,' Johnny Banton told them quietly. 'Ric Cornell will lead. Now stay close . . . our latest word is there ain't been a *vaquero* seen in this neck of the woods for weeks. But don't bet on it bein' clear. Keep your guns handy. If they want to talk, let 'em, but don't shoot unless you have to. The Mexes tend to send a whole passel of *vaqueros* when they bother to send any at all. So, if they're there, they'll have the greater firepower. All we can do is make a run for it and hope we get across the Rio ahead of their lead. OK?'

They rode in silence after that, strung-out, those near the rear more nervous than those up front behind Cornell and Banton. Jordan was trailing some but he looked around calmly, took his time, making sure shadows he thought had moved had been nothing to worry about before moving on. It earned him a few curses from the more nervous riders but he said nothing: he preferred to play things safe, always had.

If Waco Shoebridge hadn't put a bullet in him and snatched the payroll strongbox that time, he would never had served any time in prison, but he had been mighty careful since getting out, playing things as safe as he was able.

Which is maybe why he had a nagging worry about Mandy now plaguing his thoughts as he followed the band of rustlers deeper into Mexico.

He hadn't liked leaving her alone at the trading post. Sure, there were other folk in the valley but they were miles away and if she needed help . . .

She was a little afraid of the Indians, he knew, had been ever since he had bought the place. But the Indians usually slipped in and slipped out again like shadows, doing their business and high-tailing it back to wherever they hid out when they broke out of the reservations for a taste of the old life.

If they pulled off this sortie tonight successfully, that would be fine, and he would keep his word, sell up and try to find a small ranch close to a town she liked where she could socialize with other settlers and their families.

But he wished he hadn't had to leave her alone there at Fadeaway's Fare.

He realized suddenly that the bunch were reining down and he stopped the buckskin.

Banton came down the line, talking quietly. 'Muffle your mounts' hooves,' he told each man. 'Beyond that ridge lies the cattle. Cornell's scouted ahead and it looks all clear. Check your guns one last time. We move in ten minutes. Good luck, *amigos*!'

★ ★ ★

Mandy Jordan had tried to hide her anxieties and worries from her husband.

She knew he was caring enough and sensitive enough to have realized she didn't really like living in the isolation of the trading post. But she was prepared to put up with it because it would be safer for Jordan. They were married under his real name by a roving Mexican *padre* in the ruins of an old Spanish church just outside of Uvalde at the foot of the Balcones Escarpment not long after she had run off with him from Diamondback Creek. Afterwards, they had drifted through idyllic days in rich Big Bend country that he knew intimately, then headed into west Texas.

They had tried their hand at ranchwork; Jordan — now using the name of Chris Franklin — working the range while she had taken on the cooking chores. It worked out well enough but twice there had been incidents with drunken cowpokes making nuisances of themselves and pawing Mandy.

They had gathered together a little money and with what she had brought with her, there was enough to buy old Fadeaway's trading post. Mandy had tried to sound enthusiastic about it because she knew that Jordan constantly worried about being recognized by his enemies when they were close to civilization.

But she hadn't been prepared for the Indians.

Drunks she felt she could handle, drunk white men, that is, but the Apaches who cut loose from the nearby reservations were still more than half wild and she had developed the fantasy that they were after her scalp with its mass of golden hair. She had once seriously thought of cutting it off, but Jordan had caught her in time and in a fit of tears and shaking anger she had told him how she hated the place, and, as usual, he had tried to comfort her as best he could. That was months ago and she knew it bothered him and she was sorry she had mentioned her fears. But now he was taking steps to give them both a new life.

She did not approve of the way he was going about it, but if it got them away from this place and back somewhere she could chat to other women of her own age and interests . . .

She stiffened suddenly, lying in bed alone, hugging Jordan's pillow to her. *What was that?* She lay there fearfully, heart hammering, waiting again for the sound she had heard.

What kind of sound was it? She tried to remain cool, examine what she had heard, began to relax when the rasp of the warm border nightwind caressed the weathered log sides of the post. *That's what it had been!* Only the rising wind disturbing some loose item — maybe one of the old tin washtubs hanging by its iron handle from a peg on the outside wall above the bench. Or that warped window shutter on the store-room that never did close properly. It could even be some loose shingle. Yes, it had been the wind.

She was just dozing off when she jerked awake again, half-sitting up this time, eyes wide and straining in the darkness.

What was that?

It seemed to come from the kitchen. *Inside* the kitchen. No wind could have caused that sound!

Oh, dear God! There it was again. *Inside* the trading post . . .

She forced herself out of bed, reluctantly taking the single-barrelled Ithaca shotgun with her. Her knees were shaking and she almost collapsed when she pushed open the kitchen door and there, in dim reflected light, saw two rats gnawing a hole in a bag of sugar they had obviously knocked off the deal table.

The night passed with similar incidents, Mandy starting at every sound. By the time dim light oozed its way into the bedroom, she felt wrung-out and had a headache from lack of sleep.

She dressed quickly, went through to the kitchen and took a pail from beside the door. There was still only dull greyish light outside but the birds were singing and the creek was chuckling over the rounded stones of its bed, a thin mist lifting from the still pools.

That water would be icy cold under the shadowed trees at this time of day, she knew. She would bring up a pailful to the house, dip her head in and wash her hair. *That* would wake her up. She would wash her hair for Jordan.

Smiling, humming a tune, much happier now it was almost time for Jordan to return from Mexico, she knelt by the creek, leaning down from the bank to dip the pail in the running water. She grunted with effort as she lifted it up, standing, leaning over some to counter-balance the weight.

Still humming she glanced around at a flutter of birds from across the creek and felt her heart slam up into her throat.

Standing across there, the mist surrounding him and giving him a ghost-like appearance, was a tall Indian with a scarred face.

Standing as still as a statue, she

watched in growing horror as he raised his empty left hand, pointed a forefinger at her and flicked his thumb like a falling gun hammer.

Then he bared his teeth in a tight smile and began to wade the creek towards her. Her screams set the birds to flight.

★ ★ ★

It had been a good night's work, thought Jordan, along with Cornell and Banton and the others. They must have rounded-up over 200 head and picked up another hundred while driving them north towards the Rio, the stupid beasts just ambling down and joining the others being hazed along.

Banton reckoned he could sell at twenty dollars a head to the army so each man would make a decent profit. Jordan began to calculate his share as they urged the herd through a slope-walled pass, travelling back to the Rio by a different trail to the one they had used earlier.

The cowboys were all in a good mood and cut loose with a couple of somewhat muted rebel yells as they rode around the moving herd, hazing along with stragglers.

There was light streaking the sky, curled-smoke strands of gunmetal blue and rose-pink with tints of gold as the sun began its daily climb up the arch of the cloudless sky.

The pass was still in shadow, though, deep shadow, as were the slopes.

Which might explain why no one saw the *federales* and *vaqueros* at first until bunches of them appeared, sweeping down both slopes and behind the Americans, catching them neatly in a trap.

The rustlers began to close in around Cornell and Banton and the younger rancher lifted a hand. 'Take it easy. There's still a chance we can talk our way outa this!'

'Hogwash!' snapped Ric Cornell. 'These *hombres* ain't gonna palaver.

They're loaded for bear and I reckon they aim to teach us *gringos* a lesson we ain't gonna forget in a hurry — those of us who live, that is!'

'Cornell, no!' Banton shouted as the older rancher brought his rifle up to his shoulder and suddenly the pass was filled with the roar of gunfire seeming to shatter the beauty of the sunrise.

Two *federales* in their mustard-coloured uniforms, pitched from their mounts, bodies rolling and skidding down the gravelly slopes. Dust clouds rose all around the Mexicans as they skidded their horses, and that dust was punctured with gun flashes as they raked the Americans, their Mauser bolt-action rifles cracking like a dozen whips.

There was nothing else to do but for every man to look out for himself and to make his run for the border. Forget the cattle, ride like hell for the Rio and get back on to American soil where a man would be safe . . . hopefully.

'Stampede the cows through!' roared

Jordan, already riding like the wind, leaning over to one side of his racing buckskin, rifle held out for balance in his right hand.

Lead whipped through the air about him, kicked dust and stones around his mount's thundering hoofs. He swept in on the scattering cows and sat upright, working lever and trigger on his Winchester, shooting at the animals on the edge of the bawling herd.

Two went down thrashing, a third ploughing nose-first into the gravel and knelt there as if sleeping. The other steers swung wildly away from what they saw as a new menace and began to run. Jordan thundered after them, shooting from horseback, terrorizing, yelling insanely, barely noticing that Banton and some of the others were stretched out either side of him doing the same thing.

The *federales* were shouting and breaking up at orders bawled frantically by their officer. The *vaqueros* were making their own move, coming in two tight-knit bunches, trying to force a wedge beween the cowboys and the stampeding herd.

The soldiers were scattering wildly now as the herd thundered down upon them and the red-faced officer ceased bawling, his voice breaking with effort, knowing it was no use trying to keep any form of order right now. He jumped his wildeyed black mount back up the slope, trying to get above the heaving backs of the terrorized cattle.

Two soldiers tried to follow him, but, looking back instead of watching where they were going, they cannoned into each other and both men fell, rolled back down the slopes, screaming and tearing loose their fingernails as they clawed at the dirt in an effort to stop their slide.

Too late. They disappeared under the mangling hoofs of the panicked herd.

The other soldiers had forgotten all about the *gringos*, concentrating only on getting out of the pass with whole skins. But the Texans hadn't forgotten them — knew they still had to get all the way back to the border and across the Rio before they could afford to relax.

Guns hammered and cut down the men in the yellow uniforms, some mortally, others wounded less seriously. Some of the Mexicans put up a fight and two cowboys were punched from their mounts, one hitting hard and rolling lifelessly for several yards before sliding to a stop. The second tried to get to his feet but he was only yards away from the herd and he disappeared beneath the sea of heaving backs and tossing horns. Any sound he may have made was totally drowned out.

The *vaqueros* now made their move, coming in with sixguns blazing, *sombreros* whipped off their heads by the wind of their passage to dangle by their throat ties. Jordan felt the heat of a bullet touch his face lightly, instinctively wrenched aside, the buckskin giving a protesting whinny as it almost lost footing. He swung the smoking rifle around, getting the butt against his shoulder, firing one-handed. He jammed the reins between his teeth, spun the rifle around the lever to reload and whipped out his Colt pistol. Both guns blazed at the line of *vaqueros* seeking to isolate him. One man reeled and hauled his mount away, hanging over to one side. Another reared up in his stirrups, rolled backwards over his horse's rump. A third clawed at a bloody face and pitched to the ground. The man behind him wrenched his reins but his horse rode over the downed man. Jordan shot the rider out of the saddle, burst through the line of *vaqueros* and swung the buckskin back into the pall of dust kicked up by the stampeding herd.

He felt the slope beneath the buckskin's hoofs, lifted the animal, figuring to ride above the remnants of the herd and swing down into the pass beyond it.

Something reared up in front of him suddenly and he caught the glint of tarnished gold braid on a peaked cap and the shoulders of a yellow uniform, and then both horses collided. The thud was loud in Jordan's ears and he felt pain in his left leg as it was crushed between the two whinnying mounts. Then once again he glimpsed the flash of that braided cap and something smashed across the side of his head and the world exploded as he felt himself falling a long, long way . . .

He awoke to the crash of a gunshot and blinked his eyes open, trying to push upright. He felt coarse gravel beneath his hands and reeled as pain and dizziness set his head spinning. Nearby, a Texan spilled awkwardly to the ground.

'Easy, *amigo*.'

He recognized Banton's voice and felt strong fingers digging into his upper arm. He held his throbbing head, sitting there on the gravel slope of the pass until a shadow blocked off the light.

It was full day now and he saw several dead cows and horses strewn about the pass, the bodies of men, also, some mangled. He tilted his head to look up at the man standing between him and the sun, squinted as light burst brilliantly from braid on a narrow cap peak. The man held a smoking pistol.

'*Madre de Dios*! It is you!' the officer hissed.

Jordan blinked again, aware there were armed men standing behind the officer, and then he saw the narrow face with its dark beard-shadow and long sideburns, the patch over the left eye and the twist to jaw and mouth where old scar tissue writhed.

'Captain — Salazar?' Jordan rasped, clearing his throat, aware that Banton was frowning at him.

'You know this *hombre*?' the rancher asked, but before Jordan could reply, the Mexican said, with a sharp little bow, 'It is now *Colonel* Salazar, *Señnor* Jor-dan. I am *director jefe* of this *provincia* . . . ' He touched his eyepatch. 'It has been a long time, señor.'

Jordan nodded slowly. 'You lost the eye?'

'*Si*. I could use a glass one but this

patch and these . . . ' He smiled tightly as he touched the scars on his jaw and mouth. 'They serve to lend my authority some real weight. I seldom have to give an order more than once. And I have the best record for collection of taxes in the entire Mexican Federal Army.'

Jordan could believe it: the man had always been ruthless when he had known him before.

'I think you were warned never to come back to Mexico, Jor-dan,' Salazar went on slowly. 'The order was you were to be shot on sight. Yet you are here, stealing a few miserable cows from Don Eustacio Favor . . . eh?'

Jordan forced a smile. 'As long as they are only a few miserable cows, perhaps you will be agreeable for me and my pard to — ride on to the border, Colonel?'

Salazar's scarred face was sober as he looked at the silent, battered and dusty Banton with his one good eye. 'Your *amigo* eh?'

Jordan nodded. 'We have a small spread north of the Rio. We thought Don Eustacio would not mind if we used a few of his cattle for the basis of our herd.'

Salazar smiled thinly. 'Ah, so. Don Eustacio lives in Mexico City, up in the mountains where it is cool and pleasant. He has never even seen this part of his holdings, I think. But he is a fine reader, that one, and he reads his *segundo*'s tally books very, very closely. He would know if even two cows were missing from his herds. He is *muy importante*, eh?'

'Well, seems like we made a mistake, Colonel,' Banton said abruptly. 'We're mighty sorry about that. We were given to understand these were herds no longer of interest to Don Eustacio.'

Salazar looked coldly at Banton. ' 'Given to understand', *señor*? Of course, but did anyone give you *permission* to remove these cattle? I think not. You are a thief, *señor*.'

There was no answer to that and both

Texans remained silent.

'But . . . you may go.' He bowed slightly to Jordan. 'You understand, Jor-dan.'

'*Muchas gracias*, Colonel . . . I won't forget this.'

'Of course not — as I have not forgotten it was you who gave me my life that other time. But, *amigo* . . . ' Salazar shook a brown finger under Jordan's nose. 'Never, never return to Mexico, or I will personally shoot you. *Personally*. There will be no more chances. You come here again, you must be prepared to die. I will see that everyone under my command knows this. *Comprende?*'

4

Gone!

They wasted no time getting back across the Rio. Salazar had given them their guns, but with only one cartridge for each.

Now, safe again on US soil, they spurred away into the nearest brush, found a dry wash and followed it and climbed out onto a barren flat that led to sun-blasted foothills. Here there was an arroyo where they at last paused to draw breath.

Jordan noticed that Banton's hands shook as he rolled a cigarette.

'Who was that Mex colonel, Chris?'

'I got mixed up with some gun-runners a few years back,' Jordan said quietly, a little edgy, because he knew Mandy would be worried that he wasn't home by now. 'Actually, I supplied the wagons, had me a small freight business operating out of Del Rio at the time, used to run down into Mexico to some of the northern villages. I did this deal with a feller named Loomis to take along a couple of crates supposed to hold farming tools. I was dumb enough to believe him. Once across the Rio we were hit by *federales* — under Salazar, who was only a captain then.'

'There was a fight?'

Jordan nodded, remembering the way Matt Loomis had whipped out a hideaway gun from his sleeve and fired it directly into Salazar's face, the bullet ripping out the corner of his left eye socket.

Then all hell broke loose and one of Loomis' men came up with some dynamite and blew down the walls of the narrow pass where they had been jumped.

'Salazar's horse went down, crushed, pinned him by the leg. Loomis and those of his men still alive vamoosed, but I took time to drag Salazar free and tie a bandanna around his head, over his eye wound. As I was leaving, some of his men who'd survived the explosion were coming over the rocks by then. He said, 'I will remember you, Jordan.' ' He shrugged. 'Thank God he did.'

He stood now, flicking away his still burning cigarette. Banton looked up, puzzled.

'What's your hurry?'

'Mandy'll be worrying — '

Banton nodded, looked up from his cigarette end. 'There's just you and me out of a dozen men, Chris. That Mex was shootin' my men one by one when you came round . . . ' He smiled crookedly. 'Obliged you did or I'd be lyin' back there with Cornell and the others. Just one thing, Chris. He called you Jordan and you just used the name, too.'

Jordan gave him a level stare. 'That's my real name, John.'

Banton held his gaze, dragged on his cigarette and ground it out, all without looking away. He climbed slowly to his feet. I'll still call you Chris Franklin. I guess that's what you want?'

Jordan nodded. 'Thanks, John. It's best that way.'

'Fine with me. I owe you plenty, *amigo*.'

They rode out of the arroyo and made their way back to the trail that would take them to their valley. It was a hot, thirsty ride and neither man felt easy with only one bullet in his weapons.

It was past mid-morning when they approached the valley from the trading-post end and Jordan had to consciously hold back from spurring the weary buckskin forward. He was anxious to see Mandy now even though the news he had was all bad. But she was an understanding woman — although she was bound to be disappointed that they would not now be able to move out and buy a small ranch.

He had made up his mind on the long ride back that he would sell the post anyway, maybe move into Kincaid and take a job for a spell — McLeod of the general store had told him any time he wanted a job he'd be happy to give him one. They could save hard, put some of his pay with whatever they got for the post, and have enough for a small spread in a year.

He grunted involuntarily as they came over the last hogback rise and he reined down sharply, drawing a whicker of protest from the buckskin. Banton, riding close behind, head down so his hat brim shaded his face, swore softly as he hauled his mount quickly aside so as to avoid a collision.

'What the hell, Chris . . . ?'

The rest of his words choked in his throat.

Below, the trading post was a still-smouldering heap of blackened timber and smoking piles of animal hides.

Even from here they could see the charred shafts of several war arrows protruding from fire-blackened posts that somehow still stood upright.

By the time Banton rode back with a couple of grim-faced cowhands, Jordan's clothes were covered in soot and charcoal as was most of his exposed skin.

His clothing smouldered here and there where glowing timbers he had hurled aside had brushed against the cloth. He didn't seem to notice. Nor did he show any sign he knew his hands were blistered and torn from his wild search through the rubble.

His eyes had a kind of madness in them now as he glanced up at Banton and the other men from up valley.

'She's gone, John! Not a sign of her!' Jordan, swaying, swept his arm around, staggering with fatigue. 'No body — nothing. She's gone. We'll have to search the brush and that stand of timber yonder.'

He stumbled away from the charred remains of the trading post, staggering towards the brush. Banton set his fresh mount between Jordan and the vegetation.

'It's a waste of time, Chris.'

'No, she could be lying there. She might be hurt . . . '

He staggered again as he cannoned into Banton's horse as the man used the animal to crowd him back. Jordan's black-streaked face snarled. 'Get the hell outa my way, damn you!'

'Chris! *Chris!* You won't find her, man! She ain't here.'

Jordan's eyes pinched down. 'What d'you know about this?'

'Hey, whoa, *amigo*! I was with you, remember? Judas, Chris, calm down, man, take it easy while I explain.'

Jordan frowned and lowered the fist he had been about to swing into the side of Banton's horse. 'Explain.'

Banton nodded. 'My spread's been hit, too. Some other ranches in the valley as well. Mandy is the only one missin' but they shot some of my steers, run off a few others. Same with the other places.'

'Who did?' Jordan's smoke-coarsened voice was barely audible as he glared wildly into Banton's face.

'Bunch of bronco Apaches. Seems Wolf Taker was leadin' 'em. It's a big break-out from the reservation. The army's already searching for tracks up the valley. That's the way they went. Started at your place and . . . '

Jordan frowned. He was silent for a time, then he nodded slowly. 'She was always more scared of Wolf than the others, said he wanted her hair on his lodgepole. I treated it as a joke.'

Banton and the others moved uncomfortably in their saddles as Jordan hung his head, hands balled into fists down at his sides. Then he raised his face again.

'But it was no joke, was it? That son of a bitch *was* after her hair! You bring any ammunition, John?'

'Yeah, I collected some at the ranch. But, Chris, the army's up the valley. Best let them handle this.'

'Like hell I will. You said that no one

else is missing?'

Banton flushed. 'No. Sally Barrett was killed, though. Her kids hid up the chimney till the Injuns were gone. Cornell's place was burned: he always was mighty rough on the Injuns. A man dead at the Cardwell place. Mostly the rest was burned barns and some cows stolen.'

Jordan scrubbed a hand down his face, leaving pale streaks from his clawed fingers. 'The main object was to take Mandy then — ' He snapped his gaze at Banton. 'You said she wasn't here as if you knew for sure, John.'

Banton nodded. 'Wolf Taker's bunch was spotted headin' for the hills. Mandy was with 'em. Leastways, Joe Huckabee said he recognized her golden hair.'

Banton's voice trailed off. Jordan reached up, dug steel fingers into the man's thigh. 'What else?'

'Nothin'. Joe recognized Mandy's hair, that's all.'

'What?' Jordan insisted, teeth bared, fingers digging in.

Banton winced in pain. 'He — he did say at that distance he wasn't so sure whether it was — Well, Joe didn't really see Mandy, just her hair. Aw, but look, Chris, Joe's old and he don't see so well . . . '

'John, I want a fresh horse from you and some supplies and ammo. I'll take the buckskin as a spare.'

'You can't go after 'em alone!'

'You gonna get down from that claybank or am I gonna haul you outa the saddle?'

Banton drew his sixgun, cocked the hammer. 'It's fully loaded now, Chris. Now you back off, man! We stick together in this valley. I figured you'd been here long enough to figure that. We all lost somethin', we've all got us some kinda stake in this. You come back to the ranch with me and get cleaned up and have some grub. And I'll supply the bullets and the hosses and the trail grub. We'll all help. You savvy, Chris?'

Jordan stared up at him for a spell, then stepped back and nodded jerkily.

Then his legs gave way and he sat down on the ground amongst the charred timber, holding his head in his hands.

* * *

By the time the avenging posse took to the trail again, Jordan's first paralysing, unnerving shock had worn off.

It had been replaced by a cold, implacable rage that he had never felt before. Murderous thoughts swirled through his head — not one Apache in that band of raiders would live. He swore it to himself and upon the vision of Mandy's golden hair. If old Joe Huckabee *had* seen that silken hair on Wolf Taker's lance, then that Indian was going to go to meet *Ysin*, his Creator God, in a hundred pieces. He couldn't bear the thought that Mandy was dead, but his rage was cold enough to allow him to plan a terrible vengeance against any man who had been involved in her death if that should be the case.

If she was still alive . . . His mind

blocked off there. Only once had he ₁.. a chilling thought slip through: maybe it would be better if she were already dead.

It was a grim-faced, bleak-eyed Jordan who rode at the head of the eight or ten riders as they made their way up-valley, hoping to catch up with the army troop who were already trailing the bronco Apaches.

Banton had given up trying to talk to him: the rancher had furnished Jordan with fresh clothes, some spares, even, ammunition for his guns and cartridge belt, food for his grubsack, and a fresh mount, a big bay. Jordan let his buckskin trail along behind, aiming to switch from one mount to the other so as to cover more ground. But he didn't want to talk.

The other men were from valley spreads, survivors of the Indian raids, men with their own vengeance burning in their hearts.

But Banton could see no one was ever going to match the ruthlessness he saw building-up in Chris Jordan. Funny that, the way he had found out that Franklin wasn't his real name.

The hell with it, he thought. Out here you took a man on his word: he was free to call himself anything he wanted and you judged him by his actions if you took time to judge him at all. Everyone in the valley liked Jordan — and Mandy — had them figured as a quiet couple who liked to be mostly by themselves. There was no crime in that.

'Soldiers, Johnny!' one of the riders behind called and Banton hipped slightly, saw the man's pointing arm, and swung back.

Jordan had already seen the guidon coming up over the rise and turned the bay in that direction, the buckskin following willingly.

The troop came riding over the crest and kept on coming. Banton lifted his hand for the group to wait at the foot of the slope but Jordan kept on riding, met up with the officer in charge almost at the halfway mark.

The soldiers reined down, looking dusty and hot and weary. The officer was a Lieutenant Storm, about thirty, and although he was unsmiling and serious, Jordan had the notion the man hadn't had a lot of experience with Indians — except on reservations.

It turned out he was right. It took him and the others twenty aggravating, frustrating minutes to learn that the Apaches had split into two bands now, one large, heading in the general direction of the distant Staked Plains, the others going due south.

And that Lieutenant Storm intended to return to his fort for reinforcements before pursuing the larger band. It was his notion that the smaller group were heading for the border and would reach it before he could catch up to them, no matter what he did. Jordan began riding up-slope, past the weary troopers, before Storm gave the orders for his men to ride on down the ridge.

Banton wearily waved the others on to follow Jordan.

He didn't catch up with Jordan until the man was on the crest.

'You ever see such a damn fool?' he snapped at Banton, staring down at the troop now riding at a lope across the plains.

'He's green, is all. Chris, we're likely gonna need the army in this before we're through.'

'I won't need 'em.' Jordan flicked his stony eyes to the rancher. 'I won't need anyone. I've got the rest of my life to get this chore done and I won't rest until it is.'

He swung the sweating bay around and started down the far side of the ridge, scanning the trail ahead for tracks, cursing the green lieutenant for having ridden back over any sign Wolf Taker's band might have made.

*　*　*

There was a trail and only a man like Jordan could have discovered it.

Wolf Taker's band had been mighty

careful not to leave any sign but they had slipped up in a couple of places. And they obviously didn't figure on a man who had spent years after the war living with the Comanche and Kiowa searching for their spoor.

Jordan soon took over leadership of the posse from Banton, the rancher stepping down willingly enough when he realized Jordan's tracking abilities were far superior to his own. Jordan led them on a winding route that zigged and zagged through some of the roughest country anywhere in West Texas, but always came back to a line that would take the fugitives due south.

'Well, where d'we go from here?' Banton swept an arm about him. They were in rugged, stony hills, a narrow, knife-edge pass cutting through them. 'We go through the pass?'

Jordan shook his head. 'We go over.'

'Hell's teeth, Chris! That'll kill the horses!'

'We rest 'em up here till dark, then cross in the cool.'

'Man, that'll only be harder still! We go through that pass, we'll be on the other side of the range in a few hours.'

'If we get through.' Banton frowned and Jordan said wearily, 'They could be waiting for us. There's sign that some might've broken away from the main group back a'ways. I can't be sure.'

'Hell, Storm said the breakaway band was only ten or twelve men! We can handle that even if they're all waitin' in there!'

The others agreed, impatient to tangle with the raiders, unwilling to listen to Jordan's cautions. It was strange that likely he was the one man there who wanted to catch up with Wolf Taker quicker than any of the others, yet he was the one who wanted to go slow.

In the end they took a vote and, of course, he lost: they were taking the pass.

Jordan knew it was no use arguing. He checked both rifle and sixgun, mounted and led the way into the shadowed pass. He pushed his hat back and let it dangle behind him by the rawhide tiethong so he could look above and ahead more easily.

Every man in the posse did the same, all rifles on their knees, ready for instant action.

And still the Apaches caught them unawares.

Instead of setting-up their ambush on the high rim or just below on the walls, they were waiting amongst the tumble of large rocks at the base of the pass walls, hidden by the deep shadows of late afternoon.

They seemed to rise out of the ground itself — and the way dust spilled from the shoulders of a couple, Jordan later figured they must have dug shallow trenches and covered themselves with a layer of dirt. There were more than Jordan would have expected, at least ten, and they came up shooting their old rifles and deadly bows. An expert with one of those horn-strengthened hunting bows that could drive an arrow clean through a running buffalo, could get off a dozen shafts a minute. So the air was suddenly full of cracking bullets and hissing arrows with metal tips — and screaming men as these missiles found targets.

Horses reared and whinnied. Men yelled as they were smashed or tossed from the saddles. Guns thundered. Dust filled the narrow pass in a thick yellow-grey fog. Shapes leapt about like air-borne wraiths. Blood-curdling yells echoed from the steep walls.

Jordan's cheek was bleeding where an arrow-head had sliced open the flesh. He gripped the bay with his knees, the buckskin's rein ends clamped between his teeth, as he worked lever and trigger, shooting wildly with his rifle. He quickly realized he was wasting ammunition, sheathed the Winchester and palmed up his Peacemaker as he heeled the bay forward.

A shadow hurtled off a rock, crashed against the bay's neck and fell away. The horse reared with a terrible, high-pitched scream and even as he fought to stay in the saddle, Jordan heard the jetting of blood from a severed artery.

He rolled away from the direction of fall as the bay went down, stepped almost lightly to the ground, jumping aside as the crouching shadow came at him this time — or maybe he was trying for the buckskin. But Jordan crouched and the sixgun thundered twice and the Indian twisted in mid-air, arms flailing as he fell.

Jordan whirled at a sound behind and above. Another Apache was leaping at him off the top of a rock. He dropped to one knee, triggered, saw the body jerk. The Indian flopped close beside him, tried to push up, his chest streaming blood. Jordan kicked the twisted face viciously, whirled as someone screamed in mortal agony.

He saw an Apache rising from a writhing shape on the ground, blood dripping from a knife blade. He straightened his arm, ramming the hot barrel of his Colt against the back of the man's head and dropped hammer.

Something smashed into him with the force and strength of a mountain lion and he was borne to the ground. He smelled the man as his body crushed against his face and then he reached up instinctively, caught the descending knife arm. He slammed his sixgun savagely against the man's head, kicking out from beneath the unconscious body.

The man-yells were dying away but the horses still snorted and whickered and reared.

Panting, Jordan clambered to his feet, waiting for the dust to lift and show what lay beneath.

He was almost afraid to look.

But the Apaches had had enough. They had struck savagely and devastatingly and now they faded away as quickly and as silently as they had appeared. Jordan glimpsed some riders high up, but there was no flash of golden hair amongst them. He emptied his sixgun in frustration as they disappeared over the crest, looked around for the buckskin, but it and the other mounts that had survived were bunched together way back at the end of the pass. He knew if he ran down there yelling, they would all scatter out on to the plains.

He was surrounded by dead or wounded men. At least three of the ranchers' posse were dead, and every one of the others, including Banton, were wounded.

Even before he reloaded his gun and then went forward to help, Jordan knew this was trail's end for these men. They would have to return for treatment of their wounds.

From now on, he would be hunting Wolf Taker alone.

And that suited him fine.

5

The Gang's All Here

He knew they were out there in the dark.

They would expect him to set up a decoy camp — which he had done — and they would look for him amongst the rocks and the sparse timber upslope from where he had rigged his bedroll to look as if he were sleeping in it, just beyond the glow of the dying fire.

So he set up a second decoy amongst the rocks.

He used the buckskin's nosebag and some sheets of an old newspaper to make the silhouette of a man's hat, set it above the tree limbs and deadfalls he had fashioned into the shape of a sitting man, using some of the spare clothing Banton had given him.

Then he had climbed a tree about five

yards away, slightly below the place of the second decoy. He settled in amongst the branches, having cut brush to set around his limb so as to give him more cover. Indians didn't just make a habit of looking around them, they looked *up*, too, and he didn't want his shape showing against the stars.

It was two days since he had left the others at the pass. Two men were bad hit, the rest, including Banton, not too serious, but enough to keep them from a long, hard trail through this kind of country. Banton had given him more ammunition and a few dollars, which was all he had with him.

'You might need it,' the rancher said. 'It's little enough, but . . . '

The others came up with a few more dollars between them and Jordan thanked them briefly, mounted the buckskin and tossed them a brief salute on the way out of the pass.

'You send for me if you need more help!' John Banton called, nursing his shattered elbow in the crude sling

Jordan had made for him.

Jordan had waved, felt a lurch in his belly: these were good men, but he would never call on their help again. He didn't want any more dying on account of him.

Only Wolf Taker and his comrades.

He figured there were two of them creeping in on his camp as he lay perfectly still along his tree limb, trying to ignore the mosquitoes that whined around his face, occasionally drank his blood and left a stinging spot afterwards that cried out to be scratched. But he didn't move, scarcely breathed, gripping his sixgun firmly but not tightly enough to cause a cramp in his hand.

He had deliberately left his rifle with the decoy amongst the rocks. It was not loaded, but sight of it might convince the Apaches it was really him waiting there for them to fall for his camp set-up.

Anyway, a sixgun was what was needed in the kind of close combat he anticipated here.

The sliver of moon slid behind the range and he knew they would come soon now. His lips were slightly parted as he breathed shallowly, silently cursing the stub of branch that was digging into the side of his left leg. His cheek was stiff and made his face feel lopsided and the mosquitoes had now discovered the healing wound. He gritted his teeth against the stinging attack they made.

Damn! When the hell would those Apaches make their move?

They came ten minutes later, just as he figured he couldn't stand the stinging in his face wound a moment longer. He froze the movement of his hand lifting towards his wound, his ears attuned to the night sounds, hearing the faintest touch of a moccasin sole on gravel. Eyes straining to see, he waited, trying not to swallow in case the small sound was heard by the approaching killers.

Then he saw them.

Two men as he had figured, closing in on the fake figure he had set up amongst the rocks. They had totally ignored the campsite down-slope, come straight here, one from above, the other from below.

He heard the faint gasp of surprise as the first one discovered his rifle, the man unable to contain his excitement at the find. He turned it on what he thought was the sitting figure, worked the lever, and pulled the trigger. Of course, the hammer clicked on an empty breech, startling both men. Instantly they realized it was a trap but by that time, Jordan was swinging down from his tree, the sixgun blazing.

The man with the empty rifle cried out and reared back as the bullet slammed into his wiry body. The rifle clattered to the ground as he clawed at a rock, spilled across the decoy figure, thrashing. The other man dropped flat, sprang up again almost instantly and launched himself down-slope at Jordan. The Colt roared again but the Indian was coming in low, under the line of fire, grunting as he rammed his shoulder into Jordan's midriff, wrapped his arms about the white man's hips and carried him backwards.

Jordan's stockinged feet pained with the sharp gravel underneath and his legs folded. The Indian sprawled atop him, sat back, one hand strangling Jordan as he swung a war club at his enemy's head.

Jordan twisted desperately, felt his hair stir with the wind of the rawhide-wrapped club as it slammed into the ground beside his skull. He bucked and kicked, upsetting the Apache's balance but failed to break the stranglehold. He brought the sixgun around and the Indian dropped his club, grabbing at the weapon. Horny nails ripped at the flesh of Jordan's wrist. A dark, savage face lowered towards him, white teeth bared and snapping at his ear.

Jordan threw himself to the left and rolled with a mighty effort, muscles cracking. The Indian slid half off him, the hand at last coming away from his throat. Jordan kicked out, felt his foot sink into a hard belly. He snapped his head forward, bony forehead smashing the Apache's nose. The man did no more than grunt, both hands now seeking Jordan's already bruised throat. He slammed up an elbow and it landed on the gushing nose. The Apache reared back, his clawed hands out of reach for a moment. Jordan twisted away, found his sixgun, rolled on to his back and as a dark shape hurtled down on him fired twice. The body jerked upwards with each shot and he heaved the dead Indian aside, sat up, gasping, rubbing his neck as he dragged air into his aching lungs, throat hurting like fury.

His head was roaring and his breathing was just settling down when he heard a stone rattle off to his left and above him. He threw himself sideways as the bow twanged and the shaft drove half its length into the iron-hand ground beside him.

Goddamnit! They had out-smarted him. They had sent *three* warriors to get him!

The thought blazed through his mind

as he heard the bowstring draw taut with a fresh arrow. He triggered and kept triggering until the gun was empty and then he threw himself as far down the slope as he could, sliding and rolling, finally coming to rest on the bench where he had set up the fake camp.

He squirmed in behind a deadfall, hands shaking as he punched out used shells, shucked fresh ones from his belt loops. He was fully loaded in seconds — but no one came after him. No arrows sliced the night. No bowstrings thrummed.

But a man groaned.

The sound came from above him and he eased around past his stuffed bedroll, silently approaching the second decoy site. Crouching by a rock, gun cocked and ready, he saw two unmoving bodies sprawled in the wreckage of the decoy. Beyond was a slowly moving shape, crawling upslope towards the darkness of the timber. He groaned again and Jordan could see the glint of starlight on the trail of blood he was leaving on the ground. The white man bared his teeth.

Instinct drove him to his feet and he paused only to pull on his boots from amongst the debris of the decoy, then in moments stood above the wounded man. He nudged the Indian roughly in the side and the man moaned louder.

Jordan heaved him on to his back. This was the bowman and he had caught one of Jordan's bullets in the side: the broken ends of two ribs showed palely where they protruded through torn, bloody flesh.

He was very young, likely new to warriorhood. Probably he was left to hold the horses of the two assassins but had decided to buy in when he heard the shooting.

Reaching down, Jordan grabbed the man's greased hair and dragged him roughly down the slope to the campsite, dumping him beside the dully glowing campfire. He threw more kindling on, then added some twigs, saw the young warrior's pain-filled, glittering eyes watching his every movement.

He drew his hunting knife, stirred the coals with the blade, then rested honed steel in amongst them. The Indian's eyes widened as Jordan squatted beside him, still holding his sixgun.

'I dunno if you savvy much American, *amigo*, but you'd have picked up some at the reservation — so I'm telling you now, that you're gonna have a mighty hard death. Mighty hard. You've been taught that a good quick death is better than a long dreary life, but yours won't be neither quick nor good. Oh, you'll die, all right, make no mistake about it, but you're gonna take a long time. And you're gonna tell me what I want to know before you go to meet *Ysin*.'

He pulled the knife blade from the coals and the steel was already glowing red.

The warrior's dry lips parted and his eyes seemed as if they would pop from their sockets as the burning steel lowered towards his shattered side.

The rider in the ravine didn't know he was being watched.

The man on the rim turned as he heard someone climbing up behind him. A big man with dust clogging a jet-black beard which matched the long hair hanging to his wide shoulders, leaned on a rock, blotted sweat from his face with a grimy shirtsleeve and curled thick lips at the guard on the rim.

'This better be somethin', makin' me climb all the way up here in this heat.'

The guard nodded, pointed behind him while looking at the bearded man. 'Feller down at the stream in the ravine, Hal . . . waterin' himself and his hoss.'

Hal Reardon's bearded face sobered and he continued the rest of the climb quickly, stretched out on the flat rock beside the guard who was known to all and sundry as simply 'Yank'. Reardon thumbed up his curl-brim hat, squinting against the heatwaves pulsing up out of the dogleg ravine far below. 'Where?'

Yank pointed. 'Just round the bend. His hoss is hard to see against the sand bar because it's a buckskin but it's there, and the man's kneelin' to scoop up water and wash the bronc down.'

'See him now,' Hal Reardon said, as sunlight caught streaming creek water as the man scooped up double handfuls and splashed them over the horse's back. 'Rid a 'ways by the looks of things . . . '

'He keeps comin' up the ravine, he's gonna ride into our pass,' Yank said warningly.

Reardon grunted, studying the man, or as much as he could see of him. 'Give him time. He might just lead the bronc across and head on out through that other arroyo — he can see it from where he is.'

Yank nodded. 'Figured I'd better call you, though, Hal.'

'Yeah, you done right.' Reardon slid back, rolled on to his side and made a cigarette. He lit up, offered the tobacco sack to Yank who shook his head, holding his Winchester rifle in both hands as he studied the man below.

'Hal! He's mountin' up!'

Reardon dragged himself to the rim on his elbows, cigarette held down at his side, cupped in his hand. He watched for a couple of minutes then swore as the rider came into full view around the bend.

'Comin' this way, damnit!'

Yank stretched out bringing the rifle around, snugging the butt against his shoulder as he sighted along the octagonal barrel. 'Do I nail him?'

Studying the rider on the buckskin, Reardon tightened his lips, then nodded. 'Yeah — play it safe.'

Yank settled himself more comfortably, drew his bead carefully as the rider walked his mount directly towards the break in the north-west wall of the ravine that the gang called The Pass: it was no more than a twisting crevice, but it led to a screen of brush, behind which was the concealed entrance to their hideout.

'Just . . . a . . . leetle . . . bit . . . more . . . ' Yank murmured, finger curling around the trigger. Then he started and jerked his head back as Hal suddenly pushed the long barrel down hard, the butt slipping up to clip Yank on the jaw. 'Judas, Hal!'

'Just hold up. That ranny knows where he's goin'.' Reardon was up on his elbows now, craning forward to watch the man below. 'By hell, I know that *hombre*. Nah, couldn't be!'

'Who is it?' Yank rubbed his throbbing jaw, hammer lowered now. He looked sullen.

'Before your time. When Matt Loomis was runnin' things . . . If my eyes ain't failin' me, that's Chris Jordan down there.'

Yank looked at him sharply, frowned as he leaned over to see better. 'Now what in hell would *he* be doin' comin' here? Thought you told me you and the others'd been lookin' for him for years?'

'We have,' Reardon said a mite distractedly, as he watched Jordan turn the buckskin into the crevice. 'I could be wrong, but whoever it is knows about this place. We better get down there.'

They slid and slipped their way down off the rim on to the barren bench below, then took a well-worn goat track that angled downwards across the face of the slope, into the small hidden valley where they had their crude shacks and corrals containing their horses. Smoke curled from the rusted, leaning chimney of one shack. Only one man was in sight, and he was sitting under a tree halfway between the shacks and the corrals, hat tilted forward over his face, gnarled hands finger-linked in his lap, sleeping.

He jumped awake when the sweating Reardon kicked his legs, the hat falling off to reveal a bald head with lank, sweat-greasy hair dangling untidily behind his ears and down his neck. He had a wall-eye and there were scars about his mouth as if he had once had his lips smashed violently against his teeth. When he curled his lips to spit, there were spaces between his teeth where several were missing or broken off.

'The hell's wrong?' he growled.

'Visitor,' Reardon said pulling his sixgun out of his holster and checking the loads. Then he raised his voice, looking towards the shack with the smoke curling from the chimney. 'Chick — bring your Greener.'

A lean man appeared in the doorway in seconds, a sawn-off shotgun held in grimy hands. His face was long and narrow, his eyes too closeset. 'What's up?'

Reardon pointed across the valley to where the rider was visible, putting the weary buckskin towards the narrow creek. 'Recognize him?'

'From here?' Chick squinted, shook his head. 'Nah. Too far off.'

'I think it's Jordan.'

Chick snapped his head up, studying the rider again. The bald man scrambled to his feet, hand on gun butt, squinting.

'By hell, if that son of a bitch's got the gall to come back here . . . '

'Leave it till we see what he wants,' cut in Reardon harshly. 'He wouldn't be here 'less he damn well had to be. Could have trouble and we gotta make sure he didn't bring it along his back-trail.'

'He's got trouble, all right!' growled the bald man who was nicknamed, of course, Curly.

'More'n he can shake a stick at!' added Chick, tightening his grip on the Greener.

'Let him come,' Reardon said flatly, and they crowded into the tree's shade, watching the rider turn towards them. The man rode easily, a weary look to him, and although his clothes seemed faded, when he drew closer they saw that it was layers of dust that made them look this way.

And there was no doubt now about the rider's identity: it was Chris Jordan and Reardon thought that the new scar across his left cheek gave him a meaner look than he remembered.

Jordan stopped the buckskin ten feet from the group, folded his hands on the saddle horn after thumbing his battered hat back from his face. He nodded civilly.

'Gents — don't believe I know the feller with the Winchester, Hal.' Jordan jerked his stubbled jaw at Yank.

'We call him Yank. He joined us a couple years back. Not long after we heard about you gunnin'-down Tag and Ollie in Diamondhead Crick.'

'Diamondback,' Jordan corrected him. 'I'm mighty tuckered, Hal, OK if I climb down?'

'Not yet,' Reardon said, and Jordan stopped in mid-movement. 'What's along your backtrail?'

Jordan smiled thinly. 'Nothing for you to worry about. In fact, nothing at all. Haven't seen anyone for a week.'

Reardon frowned and Curly said, 'You gotta be in a lotta trouble to ride for a week just to get here.'

'Couldn't go any longer without

seeing your ugly face, Curly,' Jordan told him lightly, but he saw by the narrowing of the man's eyes that he hadn't forgotten that sixgun smashing his mouth to pulp the last time they'd met. He flicked his gaze to Chick, saw the man's knuckles were white where they gripped the shotgun. 'You'll cramp up holding the Greener tight as that, Chick.'

'I'm tryin' to stop myself pullin' the trigger!' Chick snapped, and Jordan laughed shortly.

'What d'you want here, Chris?' Reardon asked.

'Looking for Matt Loomis.'

Reardon snorted. 'Hell, he ain't run this outfit in years, I'm boss-man now. Kinda surprised to see you, but I do believe we've a few things to discuss.'

'Well, I dunno what, but I'd sure as hell like to climb down and sit on something other than a saddle. I'm getting galled.'

Hal Reardon smiled crookedly. 'Climb on down an' come in and set. I guess we can spare a cup of java and a plate of beans.'

As Jordan climbed down stiffly, he saw no welcome on the faces of the others, not even Yank, whom he'd just met. He figured they must have told him the story . . .

6

Cabezablanca

They let him eat his beans and swallow his coffee and roll a cigarette, all of them lounging about the shack on the crude furniture he remembered from years ago. It was maybe a little more rickety and a little more sweat-stained, but it was the same stuff, he was sure.

He was wary of them, for they kept their weapons on show, making it plain enough there was little friendship offered here. He fired-up his cigarette, leaned back in his chair and blew a plume of smoke to the ceiling where spiders had made a veritable web city. He decided to take the plunge.

'Gents, I've been married for a couple of years, running a trading post near Kincaid, West Texas . . . ' He let them make a few remarks about that. 'Used the name of Franklin. Made a good niche for myself and Mandy, my wife, in that valley. Made some good friends. So when trade dropped off, they invited me to join 'em on a cattle run down to Mexico — when it was an Apache moon.'

They all knew what that was, except Yank, but Chick growled an explanation, adding, 'You had yourself some trouble down that way with the *federales* one time, din' you?'

Jordan nodded. 'Ran into the same officer, Salazar, he's a colonel now and warned me off . . . but that makes no nevermind. What does, is when I got back I found Mandy had been snatched by some bronco Apaches led by one who calls himself Wolf Taker.'

Hal Reardon straightened slightly where he leaned against the wall. 'Now there's one mean son of a bitch.'

He looked a mite startled at the sharp, interested look Jordan tossed him. 'You know him?'

'We done a little business. Matt

119

Loomis sold him some guns and whiskey couple times.'

Jordan's mouth tightened. 'So I am on the right track . . . ' He murmured this only half aloud, looked steadily at Reardon and spoke in a normal voice, 'I caught one of the Injuns alive and he told me a white man bribed Wolf Taker to grab my wife and burn the trading post. They raided a few ranches in the valley as well to make it look like a random thing, but seems this white man wanted Mandy most of all. Promised Wolf Taker the latest repeating rifles and some kegs of whiskey.'

Hal Reardon frowned. 'You sayin' it was Matt Loomis?'

Jordan's cold gaze disturbed him and the knowledge made Reardon mad though he hid it well enough. 'It was a man with white hair and pale eyebrows — the Injuns called him 'Cabeza-blanca' — Spanish for 'Whitehead'.'

Curly spat on the floor. 'Well that sure weren't Matt Loomis, you blamed fool!

Matt's got brown hair and he's 'breed dark.'

Chick scowled. 'You're forgettin' that kin of his, the one from Tennessee. Pale as a ghost an' moved like one, too. He was only here once . . . '

'I never seen him,' snapped Curly and Reardon said, 'No, you were doin' time over some drunken brawl in Amarillo. Matt brought this cousin in to hide out for a few days over a shootin' back in the hills. Like Chick said, looked half-ghost. Head of hair white as a flour sack, eyebrows so pale they didn't even seem to be there. His real name was McFadden, but after a couple Mexes started callin' him Cabezablanca and he found out it meant Whitehead that's the name he used. He'd gone before you come back.'

They were looking at Jordan now and it was Reardon who asked, 'So why stick your neck out and come here lookin' for Matt Loomis?'

'Because I figured he might know where this Cabezablanca hangs out. The

Injun thought he was Loomis's brother.'

'Why would he want your wife?' Chick asked suspiciously. '*He* wouldn't know her, nor would Matt, would he?'

Jordan shook his head. 'No idea; but this Injun I spoke with swears Cabeza-blanca hired 'em to grab her.'

Reardon tugged at his beard. 'And you want our help to get her back?'

Jordan hesitated. 'I could use some help, but I really just wanted to see Loomis. If you're offering, Hal . . . '

Reardon laughed. 'By God, you got your gall, Jordan! After what you done to us!'

Jordan sighed: this was the moment he'd been dreading. 'You mean the payroll strongbox.'

He had their attention now and Chick snapped, 'By God he does! You and that goddamn Waco cleared off with it while we was left to draw the posse off you. Only neither of you showed again, till we found Waco dead way out in that canyon country, miles from the rendez-vous. We heard you was spotted up on the Pecos River. We've had the odd line on you over the years but not much since you came outa jail.'

Jordan gazed thoughtfully at the end of his cigarette. 'I'll tell you what happened.'

'Damn right you will!' Chick growled, bringing up his Greener. 'Way I figure it, you owe us ten thousand bucks! We never seen a red cent of that damn payroll thanks to your double-cross.'

'Well, I guess I killed Waco, though I never saw him die.'

'What's this!' Curly was on his feet, palming up his Colt. 'If you're gonna spill a heap of lies, you best forget it right now, you son of a bitch, or you'll be spillin' your *guts*!'

Jordan sighed, looked at each of them in turn and shook his head slowly. 'See? This is why I never came to the rendezvous. Knew you'd never believe me. Never believe that after Waco and me crossed the Spindles that he suddenly dragged iron and shot me in the back. I'll show you the scar later if you want.' No one said anything but their faces reflected scepticism if not downright disbelief. 'Thing was, I'd just started to turn and the bullet glanced off a shoulderblade. Hurt like hell and knocked me outa the saddle. Waco was already reaching for the reins of the packmule that was toting the strongbox. I was barely conscious but I got my sixgun out as he rode away and put a couple into him. Then I slid over the edge of the trail and landed in a heap on a ledge. I was stuck there for two days before I got back up to the trail and tracked down my hoss again in a small meadow.'

'You must've had a helluva lot of luck!' commented Reardon.

Jordan nodded. 'I reckon so. By that time, the posse had found enough of a trail to work their way across the Spindles and I had to make a run for it. They chased me far as the Pecos before they got me and they gave me two years in the Pen. I lost a lot of blood and hide in there when they worked me over wanting to know where the strongbox was buried. Like you, they didn't believe I didn't know. They figured Waco and me'd fought and I'd killed him and, not being shot-up as bad as Waco, I buried the strongbox in those two days I claimed to have been caught on the ledge.'

'Makes sense to me,' Chick allowed tightly, and Curly nodded. Reardon continued to glare.

'Inside, I heard that Loomis would be waiting for me when I came out so I went under cover, took a new name, tried to go straight. Have been ever since. But now . . . ' He paused. 'What happened to Loomis, anyway?'

No one spoke for a time. Finally, Reardon set his hard stare on Jordan.

'He left us, went gun-runnin' to Mexico and I heard he'd been sellin' guns to the Injuns, too — ' He paused and said quietly, 'Word is he's pards with that loco cousin of his, Whitehead.'

Jordan sighed. 'I still don't get it, but it has to have something to do with Tag and Ollie recognizing me that time in Diamondback Creek. It was a fair shoot-out but I knew I had to quit and go someplace else. I guess Loomis heard about it, started looking.' He frowned. 'If he finally tracked me down to the trading post, why did he grab Mandy? Why didn't he come in and brace me? He was always faster than me . . . '

'Forget Loomis!' Reardon snapped suddenly, startling Jordan some. 'Loomis quit on us and he don' rate too high with any of us here now. Personally, Chris, I don't give a good goddamn about your wife or why this Whitehead grabbed her.' Suddenly Reardon's sixgun was cocked and pointing at Jordan who had frozen at the table. Reardon smiled thinly. 'Know why, Chris? Because we . . . got . . . *you!*'

The others' guns came around to cover him, too, and Curly made a move as if to go around the table and relieve Jordan of his Colt but something smouldering in the man's eyes stopped him. He licked his scarred lips.

Jordan flicked his bleak gaze to them, one by one . . .

'You still think I know what happened to the strongbox, right?'

'Damn well *know* you do!' Hal Reardon said. 'And you don't ride outa here till you tell us!'

Jordan laughed harshly. 'And that'd guarantee I *never* rode out! You blamed fools! I told you what happened. It was too much of a temptation for Waco. He stole the box. He must've buried it before the wounds got to him. In which case I reckon it's gone forever.'

Reardon shook his head slowly. 'No. You're gonna tell us where you hid it.'

'Goddamnit, Reardon, didn't you hear me? I told you what happened. You can question me till hell freezes and there's nothing more I can say.'

'Want to bet?' Reardon asked, with a tight smile. 'Curly there a lot of trouble eatin' since you knocked his teeth out that time. He's been dreamin' for years about what he'd like to do.

Well, Curly, your dreams've come true, he's all yours. Where you want him staked-out so's you can go to work?'

Curly's eyes glittered at the prospect of being able to torture Jordan. He chuckled and all eyes watched as he started a wide and wary approach around the table to Jordan.

Suddenly the room seemed to literally explode in deadly violence.

Jordan lifted to his feet, kicking his chair over, the gun he had had out under the table roaring, the bullet punching a splintered hole in the table top as it angled up and across the small room to take Chick high in the chest. The Greener thundered and Yank yelled as some of the shot got him in the side. He staggered, bringing up his rifle but Jordan shot him as he arced the sixgun around, firing again as he crouched, Reardon's and Curly's guns spitting death.

He launched himself in a headlong dive under the deal table, came out rolling, Colt hammering upwards. A slug went in under Reardon's jaw and continued on to take the top of the man's head off. He was still falling when Curly yelled, made a dive for the door.

Jordan, still on his belly, wrenched around and put his last two bullets into the bald man. Curly went down across the stoop with a grunt, his pistol skidding out into the yard as he sprawled there, a thin trickle of blood snaking out from under his body.

Breathing hard and coughing a little in the thick cloud of powdersmoke, Jordan got to his feet and immediately reloaded his sixgun.

Then he went from man to man, looking for anyone with a spark of life still in him. Curly was the unlucky one. He was still breathing, though the air rattled wetly in the chest wounds.

As Jordan turned him over on to his back and dragged him into the shack, Curly cried out in pain.

'Don't be such a baby, Curly,' Jordan said, sounding indifferent to the man's suffering. 'We ain't even started yet . . .'

It was a town without law, but there were plenty of law-abiding citizens living there, trying to build a future for themselves and their families. The nearest real law was way up in El Paso, but roving rangers dropped in from time to time and made sure things weren't getting too far out of hand.

But the arrangements meant that those lawlessly inclined could set up there in Rockwall and, using the thinnest of legitimate business as a cover, apply their illegal trade more or less unhindered.

Especially with the town being so close to the Mexican border; if things got a mite too hot, a little advance warning was all that was needed and the men who didn't want to see the law simply slipped across until the rangers had moved on.

Such a man was Matt Loomis.

He had set up in Rockwall a year ago now, having noted early on that it was in a fine position for a man like himself whose business deals would not stand close inspection. Using the cover of a supply and freight business he kept the border towns well stocked with the goods they required — even if his prices were exorbitant. But as Loomis had the monopoly along that part of the border it was a case of pay up or go without, or, a third alternative was to run the risk of going after your own supplies to El Paso and passing through outlaw and renegade Apache country every foot of the way.

So Loomis grew rich on a legitimate business but it wasn't enough for a man who had been on the wrong side of the law ever since his father and brothers had taken him with them on cattle-stealing raids when he was only seven years old, his size and stealth making him an important part of their operations. Loomis had decided in those formative years that working for someone else was plumb loco: the only way a man could make his fortune on the frontier was to have enough guts and know-how to work for himself. He had both these things before he had even entered his teens and so the long years of lawlessness had begun.

There had been ups and downs, too many of the latter, and finally he had had to resort to the gun instead of his brains for some years. But now that was past: since teaming-up with good old Cabezablanca, the cousin from the Ozarks as he thought of him, things had taken an upward turn and looked like keeping on going in that direction.

Then his bodyguard, a well-built, vain man named Shawn, rapped on the door of the small, cluttered office which could produce legitimate lading bills and orders and dispatch accounts on request, and said quietly, 'There's an *hombre* out here wants to see you, Matt.' Shawn wore tightfitting clothes so that they showed off his muscles. His blond hair was combed back thickly and neatly and his moustache was a pale, symmetrical line across his long upper lip. His eyes were an attractive grey but if anyone looked deeply into them, they might recognize coldness and cruelty lurking in the shadows.

Loomis, a heavy-set man who wore his broad-cloth business suit carelessly, glanced up from the letter he was writing. The sunlight caught the edge of the stubble on his square jaw. 'Who is it?'

'Says his name's Franklin — he . . . '

Shawn stopped speaking as Loomis heaved to his feet, his beet-red face paling some. His big hands broke the wooden pen handle unnoticed. '*Chris* Franklin?'

Shawn shrugged his beefy shoulders. 'Just 'Franklin' was all he said. Claims he's an old friend.'

'Not for a long time,' murmured Loomis, teeth tugging at his bottom lip. 'All right. Show him in and you stay.'

Shawn ever alert for the possibility of violence, looked sharply at his boss. 'I show him respect or otherwise?'

'If you get my usual signal, you know what to do.'

Shawn smiled, touched his moustache with the tip of his tongue and went out. Loomis sat down again, tapping big fingers on his desk edge, then took a Sheriff's Model Colt from the right-hand desk drawer and hung it on a nail in the well of his desk where he could reach it with his right hand out of sight of whoever might be standing across from him.

He was writing again when Shawn came back and showed Jordan into the room. Loomis tried to make his glance casual but he couldn't quite hide the shock that stiffened his face when he saw his old *compadre* of the owlhoot trail.

For one thing, Jordan's Colt was pressed against the spine of the red-faced Shawn and the bodyguard's fancy, ivory-handled Colt was rammed into Jordan's belt. Suddenly Shawn was thrust forward roughly and Jordan pointed to the middle of the carpet.

'Kneel there and stay put,' he said flatly. Shawn started to round on him, face savagely angry, and Jordan hit him with the gun barrel across the jaw. The flesh opened and blood flowed and Shawn staggered. Jordan kicked his legs from under him and stood over the sprawling, dazed man. 'On your knees, hands on top of your head.'

Then in one lunging step he was in front of Loomis's desk and slashing down with his gun barrel. Loomis grunted in pain as the Sheriff's special fell from his hand, bounced off his leg and thudded to the carpet. He bared his teeth as he nursed his throbbing wrist, glaring hatred at Jordan.

'The hell're you doing, stampeding in here like this?'

'That fancy boy could hardly wait to twist my head around on my neck, Matt. It's there in his eyes. I figured to neutralize the notion before it gave birth. Where the hell did you find him?'

Loomis looked at his hang-dog bodyguard who was more concerned about the scar the throbbing cut on his jaw was going to leave than turning the tables on Jordan who now locked the office door. He stood to one side, gun casually covering both men.

'Guess where I've just come from, Matt.'

'You look like they just kicked you outa Hell.'

'Yeah, well, I've been there. Fact is, I'm still there . . . but you're gonna open the gates for me and set me free.'

Loomis frowned. 'I don't owe you anything, Jordan.'

'Wrong. You owe me the price of a trading post, but most of all you owe me my wife!'

He gritted the last word and Loomis looked mighty worried as the gun barrel snapped up to line-up on his chest. He ran a tongue around dry lips.

'Shooting me won't do you any good.'

'Nor you. Had me a talk with Hal Reardon and his boys. Curly was the only one who survived — for a time. He told me where to find you.'

Loomis was pale now. 'Judas priest! You — killed 'em all?'

'They aimed to kill me — after they'd worked on me a spell, trying to get me to tell them where that old strongbox is buried.'

Loomis snorted. 'I looked for you for years, spent a long time after you got outa jail trying to find you, wanting to get my hands on that strongbox. Then one day it hit me — your story was true. Had to be. Waco, well he'd doublecross his own mother and it was just plain bad luck in all that shooting at the hold-up that he was the one who picked up the reins of the mule carrying the strongbox. I was glad you were along . . . because you were always a kinda funny *hombre*, Chris. You were an outlaw, all right, but you had this strange code. You played it square, was what it came down to, even with fellers you didn't like. You'd give 'em an even break, take their side if they wanted a bigger share and you figured they was right.' Loomis shook his head slowly. 'Took me a long time to figure out the story you told had to the right one. Huh?'

Jordan stared back levelly. 'Didn't think you had brains enough to figure that out, Matt.'

'Had brains enough to keep you and the others alive for a few years dodging rangers and marshals.'

'I'll give you that.'

'Yeah. Well, armed hold-ups were getting too dangerous and there wasn't enough money in rustling cattle, so I decided to run a few guns over the border, sell some to Injuns who wanted 'em, make my own rotgut and sell that, too. Hal and the others weren't interested but I'm doing all right.'

'Cabezablanca your partner in all this?'

Loomis sat back in his chair, having gained a deal more confidence now. 'Whitey? Yeah. He might be a back-woods boy but he ain't dumb.'

'I'd say he is — snatching Mandy was a dumb thing to do. You'll find that out.'

Loomis's confidence drained quickly from him again. His big hands gripped the chair arms tightly so that his knobbly knuckles showed through the skin.

'Now wait up! That was Whitey's idea, not mine.'

Jordan shook his head slowly. 'Don't lie to me, Matt. You'll be more sorry than you're gonna be if you do.'

Loomis lifted a hand quickly, in a peace sign. 'It was all Whitey's idea. He owes some Louisiana riverboat gamblers nigh on ten thousand bucks . . . cheated 'em on his way down here from other trouble in Tennessee. They're catching up to him and he's met this Mex gal he wants to marry. So he figured to square the gamblers and get them off his neck. Hit me for the money and I wouldn't give it to him. We'd gotten word through some fellers who'd been doing a job for us near Kincaid that the 'Chris Franklin' who ran the trading post there was almost certainly Chris Jordan. Well, I wasn't interested in you any more, but Whitey knew about that strongbox and he figured maybe I was wrong, that you'd buried it anyway and were biding your time to go dig it up. He was taking some guns and whiskey to Wolf Taker's bunch and got the notion that if he grabbed your wife, he could use her as a lever to make you show him where the strong-box was hid.' Loomis spread his hands again. 'I swear that's the way it was, Chris.'

Jordan studied the man for a long minute and Loomis squirmed: Jordan always had been the one man who could make him break out in a cold sweat. He wouldn't look directly at Jordan's flinty eyes.

'I wouldn't take your word that the sun's gonna rise in the morning, Matt,' Jordan said slowly. 'But there's something about your story that makes me want to believe it. Now why the hell would that be? Me believing a snake like you after all the lousy things I've seen you pull over the years?'

'Because it's true!' Loomis snapped. 'It's what happened, Chris. Ask Shawn there if I didn't throw Whitey outa tl very office when he told me what he'd done. Snatching white women and holding 'em hostage might be OK in the backwoods, but you don't do that kinda thing in Texas without every man's hand turning agin you. I told him to git and if he came back I'd sic Shawn on to him.'

Jordan glanced at the now sullen bodyguard. 'I'll bet that loosened his bowels,' he said sardonically. Ignoring Shawn's look of hatred, Jordan turned back to Loomis. 'Take me to where this Cabezablanca hangs out.'

'What? You're loco. I don't do any fieldwork these days.'

Jordan's face straightened. 'Suppose I told you you were wrong . . . that Waco died right away when I shot him and I took the strongbox and buried it. And left it buried all this time. Fact, I was getting ready to sell up the trading post and dig up the payroll, then go buy a decent ranch where Mandy could have a better life — then your goddamn kin stepped in!'

Loomis studied Jordan closely. He looked cunning, shook his head. 'No, not you, Chris.'

'Why not me? A man can get sick and tired of playing square and seeing others grow rich. You take me to Cabezablanca and help me get Mandy back and I'll give you a half-share in that strongbox, Matt. You've got about thirty seconds to make up your mind, then I set fire to this place, drag you out — I won't worry about pretty boy there — and I guarantee you'll wish you'd agreed to take me to Whitey right off . . .'

Loomis was wavering and although he wasn't sure about the strongbox, he knew Jordan wasn't bluffing about burning down the building. With all the illegal whiskey and ammunition for the rifles stored down in the hidden cellar, it would take half the town off the map.

'I still reckon you never hid that strongbox.'

'Well, that's the chance you gotta take, Matt. You got about twenty seconds left.' Jordan took a vesta from his pocket and held it up with his left thumbnail ready to snap the head into flame. 'Now, which'll it be?'

Then Shawn made his move. He dived headlong at Jordan's legs, ramming into the man with his shoulder, taking him back halfway across the room.

The match in Jordan's left hand flared and he tossed it wildly aside. It landed in the waste basket under Loomis's desk and the papers in it immediately burst into flames. Matt Loomis, already out of his chair and starting around the desk, gave a startled cry and lunged for the basket, knocking it on its side, spilling the blazing papers on to the carpet which began to smoulder and flicker into flame.

Jordan kicked at Shawn as the man reared up over him and swung a punch at his head. Boots took the bodyguard in the chest and he spun away, falling, breaking it with one hand and starting to push upright again even as Jordan lunged in, swinging.

Shawn took two hard blows in the face and roared with rage. Jordan knocked him on his back, rammed a knee into the man's chest and pulled him half upright. He hammered a blow into Shawn's face and felt the nose go, gushing. Shawn screamed, more in outrage at the disfigurement it would cause him than in pain, though that was considerable. He struck blindly and one of his blows took Jordan in the groin as he straddled the man. Jordan grunted and doubled over, spilling to the side. He drew up his knees and Shawn was on top of him immediately, spittle flying as he raged curses and profanity with each blow he drove at Jordan's head. Jordan tried to straighten his legs and kick the man off but the pain in his belly was still too great. He groped blindly with his hands, felt the hot wire of the waste basket and swung it around and up, releasing it almost instantly as the metal burned his fingers.

There were still burning papers and rubbish in the basket bottom and they jarred into Shawn now, sticking to his shirt. He reared back, face contorted in terror as the cloth flared and flames enveloped his upper body. He ran blindly, screaming still, hit the window and plunged through. He was still afire as his body rolled across the shingle of an awning roof and then thudded into the street. Startled townsfolk stared in shock for agonizing moments before someone scooped up a pailful of water from the horsetrough and tossed it over the screaming bodyguard.

In the office upstairs, the curtains were ablaze now and Loomis, forgetting about Jordan, only wanting to save his office and his stored illegal stock below, tore the curtains down and threw them out into the street. Coughing in the smoke, he stamped out another burning patch of carpet, saw Jordan climbing painfully to his feet and made a dive for his Sheriff's Colt where it lay beside his desk.

Jordan's boot slammed down on Loomis's big hand as it reached for the weapon and the gun-runner squirmed and grimaced as he tried to draw away.

Jordan pressed the barrel of Shawn's ivory-handled Colt against Loomis's head.

'Leave it be, Matt.' His voice was thick and raspy from the smoke. Someone was now hammering on the door. 'Tell 'em to go away, Matt, that everything's fine — for the moment.'

He cocked the pistol and Loomis, panting, hands blistered, nodded slowly. 'OK — you win, you son of a bitch! I don't owe Whitey nothing. I've had the rangers in here because he gives guns and whiskey to them Apaches. I'll take you to him.' As Jordan released his hand and Loomis sat up rubbing it, the man smiled crookedly. 'But you better hope Shawn's dead . . . he'll never let you live after what you done to his face.'

7

Ghost Rider

They were well on their way to the border country when Jordan finally gave way to the uneasiness that had been plaguing him ever since leaving Rockwall.

It was the old survival instinct working, he was sure, the same hunch that had kept him alive through all the outlaw years. He had a feeling that he was being followed. After pausing on several occasions and checking out his backtrail, Matt Loomis laughed derisively.

'Shawn starting to bother you, Chris?'

'Someone is — back there. I've had this feeling, now I think I see a slight red haze of dust. Light's not quite right to highlight it.'

Loomis hipped in the saddle, squinting. 'Ye-ah. Might be. Bet you ten to one it's Shawn. I warned you: he won't let you get away with burning him up like that. I'll bet he started after us soon as the sawbones patched him up.'

Jordan had been carrying his rifle in his hands. He levered in a shell now, lowered the hammer. 'If he's fool enough to try anything, I'll kill him.'

'You'll have to if you want to stop him — just tell me where you stashed that strongbox first, though, eh?'

Jordan looked at the big man coldly. 'Keep riding, Matt. Longer we sit here jawing, the more danger Mandy's in.'

They rode another half-mile and Jordan was again checking out the backtrail, when Loomis said, 'How come you went and got yourself hitched?'

'Just kind of happened.'

Loomis snorted. 'Should've picked someone with a rich father.'

'I did.'

Loomis frowned. 'Then what . . . ? Ah! Didn't figure you were good enough for his daughter, right?'

148

'That's how it was.'

'Too bad. You should've dug up that *dinero* and slapped it down in front of him — I'll bet he'd have changed his mind about you then.'

'Not so sure. Miles Prendergast wouldn't be too impressed by ten thousand dollars. He spends more each season on his stock.'

Loomis arched his eyebrows. 'Hmm. Might be worth paying the sonuver a visit by the sounds of it. Big herds, not far from the border . . . '

'Forget it, Matt, just get me to this Whitey.'

Loomis looked at him steadily. 'You better not be joshing me about this strongbox.'

'That's something you'll just have to wait and find out.'

'You better not be!' Loomis repeated tightly, then set his mount down the grade.

Before urging his buckskin to follow, Jordan took one final glance back along the shadowed trail they had followed into these rugged hills. Before he thought he had glimpsed a pale patch of something moving, an animal rather than a man, but the impression he had was of a grey horse.

Loomis had told him that Shawn forked a big black.

They made camp in a narrow gulch, no fire, bedding down amongst the rocks and brush. Loomis seemed content enough to settle into sleep but Jordan was edgy, the old hunch working overtime, nagging at him.

The rocks were pale and he wondered if the bulk of their bedrolls would show up against them? There wasn't much light, a scud of cloud masking the stars. Jordan lay there, gripping his rifle under his blanket, head propped up on his saddle, ears straining, eyes watering with the effort of trying to catch any movement out there in the night.

He realized he was trying *too* hard, the strain of keeping his head partly raised causing the blood to thunder in his ears and mask any slight sounds that didn't belong to the border night. The moon was rising over the hills and a faint, though brighter, light washed over the gulch. He stiffened.

There had been a faint — very faint — sound out there, reminiscent of something metallic, though not clear enough to identify. Suppose it had been a rifle hammer cocking slowly . . .

He was rolling out of his blankets when something whacked the rock beside him, showering his blanket with a stream of sparks as the bullet gouged basalt before ricocheting away, the sound mingling with the dying gunshot.

Jordan rolled right across the prone Loomis, bringing the startled man upright in a tangle of blankets, cursing.

A rifle crashed again and Jordan hugged the ground but neither heard nor saw the bullet. Crouching beside a rock now, rifle hammer cocked under his thumb, he scanned the darkness of the ridge above, instinct telling him this was the best place for a bushwhacker.

'Get under cover!' he hissed at

Loomis who was only now struggling free of his blankets. The gun-runner kicked free, rolled across cleared ground and rammed himself in tightly between two low rocks. 'See him?'

'No.' Jordan sounded puzzled, trying to find the ambusher's position, tensed and expecting more shots at any second.

They never came. But they heard the faint drumming of hoofs on the far side of the ridge.

Jordan snapped his head around to Loomis. 'Shawn got a yeller streak?'

'No, sir! I hired him because he's pretty damn well fearless. That couldn't've been him doing the shooting. He'd've got you first shot or, if he did miss, he'd stay put until he did nail you.'

Jordan lowered his rifle hammer slowly. 'Queer, all right. Unless he sent his horse a'running to decoy us out there.'

'He might decoy you, but he ain't decoying me,' Loomis said flatly. 'You go out there if you want. I'm staying put.'

Jordan didn't reply and didn't move for several minutes. Then he said quietly, 'I'm gonna take a look.'

'Listen, where's that box buried? Just in case . . . you know?'

Jordan scowled and slipped away into the night. It was a good ten minutes before Loomis heard his name called from up the slope above the gulch.

'Get on up here, Matt! Something queer's going on.'

Loomis went reluctantly and when he saw Jordan standing by a clump of boulders looking at something on the ground, he made his way across warily.

'What is it?'

Jordan pointed to the dark shape.

'Shawn — shot through the left temple neat as you like. Rifle was still in his hands so he died instantly. His gun was cocked ready to fire. But someone up the slope nailed him first.'

'Who the hell . . . ?'

'Yeah, who the hell shot Shawn and

incidentally, likely saved my neck, then rode out without even stopping to be thanked?

There was no more sleep that night and at first light, Jordan went looking for tracks. He found where the mystery rider had staked out his horse, climbed up the slope so as to get slightly above Shawn's position, even found an empty .44 shell-casing that had held the bullet that had killed the vengeful bodyguard.

Jordan lost the trail when he reached the crest of a ridge. It had been wiped out expertly. He knew he could likely pick it up again in time but didn't see the point.

If the ghost rider wasn't hostile to them, why bother?

★　★　★

Loomis was gaining confidence the further south they rode. The second day seemed to give him a massive boost, so much so that he reined down in the midst of a dry river delta where nothing but air-currents had flowed between the eroded walls for a thousand years. He folded his hands on the saddlehorn and looked steadily at Jordan.

'I dunno that I needed to make a deal with you, Chris. I mean, if you did bury that strongbox, it has to be near where Waco was found, and there're only a few hills there with handy caves — and I reckon you'd use one of them if you had a bullet in you.'

'You're right, Matt. Not a cave, exactly but a cutbank. I collapsed it over the strongbox. Then I loaded Waco's body on his horse and dumped him miles away . . . where he was eventually found.'

He grinned as Loomis's face straightened as the man realized he didn't know as much as he thought.

'You're lying!'

Jordan shrugged. 'Believe what you like. Don't know why you're fussing. Just take me to Whitey first, then I'll show you where the box is.'

Loomis's eyes narrowed. Eventually

he sighed. 'All right, but you better . . .'

They were there in minutes. Loomis showed him a hidden entrance behind a clump of brush and it led them into more hills that had been screened by the first line. Halfway up the slope on one, set amidst trees, was a cabin, and there was a thin curl of smoke coming out of the stone chimney.

'Looks permanent.'

'Joe Indigo's old place.' Loomis spoke of a well-known border bandit and rustler of a few years back who had been hunted on both sides of the Rio by the law. Eventually a jealous woman had turned him in to the rangers but his hideout had never been discovered. Not by the law, leastways.

'Well, someone's home.' Jordan was checking his sixgun, the rifle already cradled in the crook of his arm, a shell in the breech. He looked coldly at Loomis. 'I'll do the shooting, if any. I don't want Mandy being hit by any stray lead.'

Loomis heard the tremor in the man's

voice and marvelled again that a butt-headed hardcase like Chris Jordan could go soft over any woman. She must be some looker, he concluded.

But he nodded in agreement to Jordan's words.

'I'll follow you in, only shoot if he's got some sidekicks.'

Jordan rounded fast. 'Was he riding with someone?'

'No. He was to take the shipment to Wolf Taker by himself . . . but I dunno what Whitey's been up to since I last seen him.'

'Watch my back then, and keep an eye out for Mandy.'

They left the weary, dusty, and foam-flecked mounts under some trees, went up on foot. Jordan wasn't keen on an armed Loomis being behind him but didn't see anything else for it. They drew close to the hut, smelled the smoke, saw only two horses in a pole corral behind the cabin. The shutters and door looked solid, the latter closed. Jordan swore.

It would be dangerous trying to ram through that door, get inside, straining to see in the half-light, searching for Mandy, before he even pulled trigger on this Cabezablanca.

'He might have a bar across inside,' Loomis remarked mockingly casual.

Jordan looked at him bleakly. 'OK — you kick it in. I'll be right behind you.'

'Like hell!'

Loomis stiffened as the rifle barrel swung down to cover him. 'He's your kin — call out! Go on, do it, man!'

Loomis turned slowly to the cabin. 'Whitey? It's me, Matt. You in there?'

No reply and at a jerk of the Winchester, Loomis called again. This time, after a long silence a weak-sounding voice replied, 'What you doin' here, Matt?'

'Come to see you. To warn you. Chris Jordan's searching these hills for you. Lemme in, Whitey. I'm hungry and thirsty as well.'

'Door ain't locked. You better not be

lyin' to me, Matt!'

'Hell, we're cousins, ain't we? Comin' in now . . . '

Jordan was right behind the man, so close their bodies were touching. Loomis placed a hand on the latch, hesitated, lifted it, then flung the door wide, diving to one side.

Two guns roared, the shots close enough together to blend into one. Jordan was down on one knee in the doorway, the butt of the smoking rifle braced into his hip.

Across the dim room, a man with a mop of silver-white hair was slammed back on the sacking-and-sapling bunk where he was lying, a smoking gun spilling from his hand. Jordan lunged forward. '*Man-dee!*'

Then Jordan was in the cabin as Loomis came around fast, swinging his sixgun. Jordan struck it from his hand with the rifle butt, then rammed the butt into Loomis's forehead. The man's legs folded and he dropped to his knees, swayed a moment and then spread out on his blood-streaked face on the hard-packed earthen floor.

Jordan looked about him swiftly at the crude, though serviceable furniture, the five bunks, the corner screened off by a blanket on a cord.

He lunged for it, tore it down with one savage yank — but stared into an empty corner. 'Mandy . . . ?'

Bewildered, he looked around again, even above his head, but the roof wasn't lined and there was nowhere anyone could hide or be hidden up there.

Which meant that Mandy wasn't here.

Whitey moaned and stirred on the bunk and Jordan strode across, rifle lever working as he pointed the muzzle at the white-haired man's kneecap. There was fresh blood on the man's side where Jordan had shot him coming through the door, but the words froze on Jordan's lips as he saw the man more clearly now close-up.

He had been battered and burned and cut. Someone had even partly scalped him, a strip of white hair missing down the middle, front to neck.

Jordan felt the coldness in his belly as he recognized the signs of a man who had suffered Indian torture.

'Where is she?' he whispered hoarsely. He drove the rifle barrel hard into the blistered leg and Whitey moaned. 'Where, you son of a bitch!'

Whitey had a fox-like face and his long thin nose had been deeply gashed by a honed blade. The dried blood gave his face an horrific look and only one eye was useful. Scars and blisters and twisted flesh showed where the other had been burned with a blazing brand.

'Wolf Taker's got her,' Whitey rasped. 'I-I only wanted her . . . to . . . trade for that . . . missin' . . . payroll. Weren't gonna hurt her — swear it — but Wolf Taker wouldn't hand her over to me. I tried to take her and they roped me and dragged me through a fire, had some-some devil's fun with me before . . . and they rode off — '

'They took Mandy with them?'

161

Jordan hardly recognized his own voice it was so tight and shaky and distorted.

Whitey nodded. 'Yeah. I-I was lucky to get . . . out . . . alive — '

Jordan's face hardened in the gloom. 'You may not think so by the time I'm through with you, you bastard!'

Just then Loomis came out of his daze, Whitey's pleas ringing in his ears. His heart pounded and his hand shook as he wiped sticky blood out of his eyes and felt the swelling, pounding bump on his forehead.

One glance around him was sufficient to remind him of what had happened and where he was. He sat up groggily on the dirt floor and Jordan, standing beside the bunk where Whitey writhed, glanced coldly at him.

'You want to live, you'll stay put, Matt.'

'Judas priest. What happened to Whitey?'

'Mostly Wolf, but I'm about to leave my mark on him, too, unless he tells me where my wife is.'

He swung back to the bunk and Whitey turned his disfigured face towards Loomis. 'Help me, Cousin!'

'Would if I could, Whitey, but I ain't so spry myself. Tell him what he wants to know, you idiot!'

'I do an' he'll kill me!'

'You don't and you'll wish he had. You got yourself a slew of trouble, cuz. Can't say I din' warn you.'

Jordan's hands moved and Whitey suddenly shouted, 'All right! Wolf Taker was headed for his *rancheria* down in the Sierra Mojos.'

Jordan swore. Just what he needed: a trip into Mexico!

8

The Scarred Wall

Whitey didn't live through the night. Jordan's bullet likely finished him although he had been badly injured by Wolf Taker and his Apaches.

If the Indians hadn't been so drunk on their *tiswin* and the rotgut whiskey Whitey had supplied them with, the man might never have escaped with his life. He had abandoned Mandy but after seeing the man's injuries, Jordan couldn't really blame him for thinking only of himself.

They buried Cabezablanca behind the cabin, took the two horses from the corrals as spares and whatever food was in the place.

'Obliged to you for coming along, Matt,' Jordan told Loomis as he strapped the last pack on one of the spare horses.

Loomis smiled crookedly. 'Don't have much choice, do I? If you won't take time to show me where the strongbox is, so I have to tag along and help you snatch your wife back from the Apaches. I must need my head read. I can make ten thousand in five, six loads of guns across the Rio.'

Jordan grinned. 'It's called greed, Matt,' he said, swinging aboard the buckskin. 'You always did have a powerful dose of it in your make-up.'

Loomis nodded, mounting his roan. His face was sober, his eyes hard as they found Jordan's. 'I got me a wide streak of mean, too.'

'I recall.'

'Good. Just remember it. Because if I don't get my hands on that strongbox after all this . . . '

'Guaranteed, Matt — if you survive.'

Loomis's face straightened and he sounded a little surprised as he said, 'Hell, yeah, there's that!'

They rode down the slope and away from the hidden mountain, turning south towards the border, less than three miles distant now. In fact, they could see across into Mexico from the high slopes and Jordan felt his belly tighten, wondering where Salazar was.

If they ran into him, it would be trail's end and an unmarked grave or his bullet-riddled body simply left out for the coyotes.

But it was a risk he had to take if he ever wanted to see Mandy again.

★　★　★

'You're acting mighty leery.'

Jordan glanced up at the comment as he crouched between two rocks on a patch of high ground, checking the sun-blasted land that lay ahead.

'You recall that Salazar? The one you shot in the eye with your derringer?'

Loomis frowned. 'Kind of . . . '

It was a typical answer from the gun-runner. He had always been ruthless and cold-blooded. Likely he really did have to work at remembering the shooting of Salazar that other time, so long ago.

Jordan told him about his run-in with the man on the rustling expedition with Johnny Banton. 'He gave me a chance to get back over the Rio, swears he'll shoot me on sight if he catches me on the wrong side of the border again.'

Loomis whistled softly. 'And here we are, already ten miles south of the Rio. Yeah, I see why you're acting so leery now. I guess the son of a bitch wouldn't exactly welcome me with open arms, neither.' He swore. 'Wish you'd told me earlier.'

Jordan said nothing but his look asked, Would it have made any difference?

Loomis shrugged suddenly. 'Well, I guess I'd've come anyways. You know where this Apache *rancheria* is?'

'Never been here but feller named Cornell — he was killed on that rustling run I told you about — he said he'd been with some scalp hunters years ago before settling down to ranching. He told us about a raid they made on the Sierra Mojo *rancheria* one night. I can find my way in, I reckon.'

'Finding the way out again is what counts.'

Jordan didn't bother answering and, satisfied that the country they had to cross ahead was safe enough, he mounted, checked his guns, and started forward, rifle held ready across his thighs.

It took them until sundown to make their way through the tangle of dry washes and dog-leg arroyos and Loomis was already worried about their water.

'Quit drinking so often then,' Jordan told him, unsympathetically. 'You've had the canteen up to your mouth every couple of minutes.'

'What I could use is a good stiff slug of bourbon.'

'You've grown soft, Matt. I've seen you put a bullet through a man's leg and leave him lying in desert country for filling his canteen with whiskey instead of water. You've been too long behind a desk.'

Loomis's dust-caked eyes narrowed. He didn't care for that jibe — mostly because it was mighty close to the truth.

'We still need water,' he growled sullenly.

'Quit talking so much and your mouth won't get so dry.' Jordan set the weary buckskin towards a stone-studded slope. 'There should be a spring up here. We'll top up the canteens and find a place to camp for the night.'

'How close are we to Wolf Taker?'

'He should be holed-up on the far side of the range. Coming this way, we'll be above him.'

'Judas! Why not move in tonight?'

'Dawn'll be better.'

Loomis didn't seem convinced but he put his roan up the slope after Jordan, leading the spare horses.

Privately, Loomis admitted Jordan was right: he *had* been far too long behind his desk. He was out of shape.

Worse still, he was getting a sick twist of fear in his belly at the thought of going up against these renegades. Mexes and white men didn't bother him, but Apaches . . .

The *rancheria* was hard to see in the dimness of early morning, scattered across the barren grey slopes of the rugged sierras. Campfires smouldered outside the wickiups, crude, dome-like structures built of sticks and dried grass. A few bodies sprawled in the dust, but the only movement was a pariah dog with crippled hindquarters dragging his bony body towards some morsel of food lying in the dust near the entrance to one of the wickiups.

'They dead?' whispered Loomis, crouching beside Jordan amongst the rocks above the permanent camp.

'Drunk most likely.'

'I don't see no one guarding the horses.' Loomis indicated the bunch of mustangs corralled in an area whose limits were marked out by stacked, drystone walls.

'In this country, the Apache'd rather fight on foot than from horseback. They don't put as much stock in owning horses as the Comanche or Cheyenne. They'd as soon eat one as ride one.'

'And how do we find out where she's being held?' Loomis watched Jordan expectantly.

'We check out the wickiups, one by one. We can see through the gaps in the sticks. No need to go inside.'

'Damn right there ain't! Man, I knew that was what you had in mind! Hell, I ain't so tired of living that I want to go down there, playing peek-a-boo, and find some hung-over Apache staring me square in the eye through a gap in his wickieup!'

'You want the strongbox?'

Loomis swore. 'I'm beginning to wonder if I want it *that* bad.'

'Help me get Mandy back and it's all yours, Matt.'

Loomis's face sharpened. 'All ten thousand?'

Jordan nodded. 'I don't want any part of it. I just want Mandy back.'

Loomis studied Jordan closely before nodding jerkily. 'You got a deal. I know your word's good, Chris.'

'Right — let's get on down there and find her.'

Matt Loomis felt the cold sweat break out all over his body and although he had checked his weapons less than a minute ago, he found himself doing it again, his hands shaking.

He had fought Apaches before but he had always had other men with repeating rifles to back him up, at least half a dozen. These odds didn't appeal to him, but he kept telling himself that just a few minutes of danger, then the ten thousand dollars would be his, if he lived long enough to get his hands on it . . .

He was moving forward, automatically following Jordan, and suddenly he came up hard against the man who had stopped in his tracks. Jordan crouched abruptly and, alarmed, Loomis followed suit. 'What?' he grated looking around quickly.

Jordan didn't have to answer. Below the ledge where they crouched, there was movement all around the Apache camp. Men in mustard-coloured uniforms were closing in, bolt-action rifles at the ready. They had almost surrounded the *rancheria*.

'*Federales!*' hissed Loomis. 'Where the hell'd they come from?'

'I dunno, but they're gonna get Mandy killed!' Jordan gritted. 'They'll shoot anything that moves in that camp.'

Then, before Loomis could stop him, Jordan triggered three swift shots into the air, the explosions tearing apart the peace of the sierra morning.

'*Move! Move!*' cracked Jordan, grabbing at Loomis's sleeve and hauling him back from the ledge as sudden chaos sounded down in the Indian camp.

After a stream of shouted Spanish

curses, the *federales*' rifles opened up as Indians stumbled from their crude shelters, some entirely naked, groping instinctively for weapons. Some had guns, but many had only bows and arrows. They were cut down in a withering hail of fire and women and children began screaming as the Mexicans closed in, shooting and hacking with their machetes indiscriminately. Jordan and Loomis set up in some rocks, shooting the Mexicans and Indians both, Jordan frantic to catch a glimpse of Mandy's golden hair. But all he saw were squaws, young, old, one obviously blind and cut down by a sword-stroke wielded by Colonel Salazar himself.

'Christ! That's all I need!' Jordan gritted, took a shot at Salazar but a fat soldier ran between the colonel and the bullet at the wrong moment, spun around and fell gasping and bleeding to the ground.

Salazar was beside himself, spittle flying as he screamed at his men, at the same time looking around him and up at the ridge where the two Americans crouched, shooting.

He dived for cover behind a downed horse as Jordan tried to nail him again. Loomis was reloading his smoking rifle, shaking his head.

'Judas, Chris, things sure ain't dull around you, I gotta give you that!'

Lead whined off the ledge, chewing stones, forcing both men to duck. Jordan swept his hat back, raising his head warily, yet recklessly.

'You'll get it shot off, you blamed fool!'

'I'm trying to see if Mandy's there!'

Loomis shook his head. 'Best hope she ain't,' he said quietly, and started shooting once more, concentrating on the Mexicans now for most of the Indians were either dead or wounded or running away. Some soldiers pursued them, others went amongst the dead and wounded and began taking scalps. The Mexican Government still paid bounties on Indian scalps, adult or child.

'We better get outa here!' Jordan said, and they started back up the slope but hadn't gone more than a few yards when soldiers stepped between them and their mounts, rifles levelled.

Salazar himself appeared, smiling tightly. 'Jordan! I hoped it would be you! I have a special wall waiting for you. Very special! Oh, it is a little scarred and bloodstained, but then you won't be standing before it for very long.' His voice hardened. 'Drop your guns or you will be shot where you stand!'

Jordan sighed and looked resignedly at Loomis. Then he winked and with a wild rebel yell suddenly lunged down the slope to the ledge and leapt out into space. The Mexicans froze, taken completely by surprise, and Loomis, too, was briefly stunned. Then he remembered the steep slope beyond the rim, consisting of loose scree and pulverized rock, a kind of coarse sand. He had wondered earlier how they were going to climb down without setting off slides that would seep into the village and wake the Indians.

Then he was following Jordan and as he became airborne, legs and arms flailing, seeing Jordan rolling and spilling down the slope, Salazar recovered and screamed orders and rifles cracked behind him. He even heard the bolt-actions work as fresh cartridges were levered into the breech. Then he hit, his boots digging in and his momentum throwing his upper body forward and down and next moment he was sliding and spinning in a cloud of dust and grit towards the bottom of the slope.

Jordan had already reached the bottom, staggered upright, saw Loomis was tumbling down and the Mexicans were now lining the rim. He fired several shots wildly, saw them scatter, turned and ran into the smoking village. Some of the soldiers were at their bloody butchering and he shot two down, weaved around a third as the man groped for his machete, swung the rifle by the barrel and felt the jar as it slammed across the man's head.

He heard Salazar's voice screaming orders. Guns hammered above and bullets kicked gravel around his pounding boots. Then he dived over the dry-stone wall of the corrals and the frightened mustangs inside reared and pawed and whinnied. In moments rock chips jumped from the wall and then Loomis came tumbling in, rolling and skidding, losing his grip on his rifle. Jordan, on one knee, emptied his Winchester at the rim and the soldiers up there scattered and dropped from sight despite Salazar's screamed orders.

'Hope you can ride bareback!' Jordan said, lunging at the nearest horse, a pinto, catching the flying mane and leaping on to its back in one jarring motion. He kicked the flanks and set the horse running at the wall where some of the stones had fallen away and it dipped low. As he sailed over, a few wild bullets zipping through the air, he glimpsed Loomis clawing his way onto the back of a big dun and then they were both racing away deep into the sierra.

Behind them, Salazar's orders were incomprehensible as he waved his sword and pointed and danced in frustrated fury on the rim of the ledge. His voice had gone on him and his men stared at him bewilderingly.

While they did so, the two *gringos* made their escape.

9

Slavers' Trail

Loomis wasn't happy about Jordan's plan to sneak around behind the pursuing Mexicans and get back to where they had left their horses and supplies.

'Salazar'll be throwing a fit,' Jordan explained. 'He won't even take time to look for our broncs. He'll get his men mounted and on our trail right away.'

He hipped in the saddle to look behind from where they had stopped amongst some suncracked ancient boulders. Loomis was already watching their backtrail and he silently lifted an arm and pointed to a dust cloud rising out of a dry wash they had traversed shortly before.

'Yeah, they're already coming. But we ain't gonna get away riding these mustangs, bareback, no water, no ammo or food. We *need* our own broncs, Matt. I can leave a false trail that'll send 'em on into the sierras, long enough for us to go get 'em.'

'I'm all for my own bronc,' admitted Loomis. 'But goin' back — what we gonna do when we do get 'em? We dunno where to go, what to do?'

Jordan's face was hard. '*I* know what I'm gonna do — what I've been doing for weeks. Search for Mandy.'

'Where, for Chrissakes?'

'Let's get our broncs first.'

Jordan spurred away, keeping the rocks between him and the distant soldiers who were now emerging from the dry wash. Loomis shook his head and tagged along, fighting the dun all the way. He watched from a small ridge as Jordan laid a false trail and then returned by a round-about route. Without speaking, they both rode down the far side of the ridge and began the long, circuitous route that would take them back to where they had left their mounts above the Apache *rancheria*.

It was a tense ride and they made wild dashes between cover, at the same time, trying to keep down the dust.

Twice they topped out on the high ground where they could see back along their trail. There was no sign of the soldiers and, encouraged, they increased their speed and came up on the place where they had ground-hitched their horses from above and to one side. By then they were afoot, leading the sweating horses who were glad to plod along without riders after the hard trail.

Jordan waved his rifle briefly to Loomis, indicating he should get down low. Loomis sidled up to where Jordan was squeezed in between two rocks, silently levering one of his few remaining cartridges into the rifle's breech.

'There's someone down there!' Jordan said quietly, and Loomis hissed a curse.

'I damn well knew it! Now we're back where we started!'

Jordan said nothing, strained to see

better down into the hollow. Their horses were here, all right. The man he had glimpsed hadn't moved. He frowned when he saw that it was an Indian, and the man was badly wounded, judging by the amount of blood on him. He had propped himself up between two rocks, sitting on the ground.

Jordan couldn't see him full-on and didn't see any weapons. But there could be a gun on the far side, hidden by the man's body. He made signs for Loomis to say put and started out of the rocks, crouching low, rifle at the ready. He made his way down the slope more silently and swiftly than Loomis expected and then Jordan was down behind the horses. They looked up, smelling or sensing him, Jordan's buckskin making a soft whinny of welcome.

Loomis swung his gaze towards the Indian but the man didn't stir at the sound. Must've passed out, he thought.

Then Jordan was rising out of the

rocks to one side of the Indian, rifle cocked and covering the man. He said nothing, and Loomis could see the frown on his face as he glanced towards the rocks where the gun-runner waited.

'C'mon down, Matt, he's dead.'

Loomis was panting and sweating by the time he reached the dead man and he started as he looked at the Indian, following Jordan's pointing rifle barrel.

It was obvious the man — wounded in the attack on the camp — had been dragged here and tortured. Or tortured first and then dragged here. There was a note pinned to his chest with an Indian knife, the blade driven in deep.

'God almighty!' Loomis breathed, a man who was no stranger to administering torture when necessary. 'This poor bastard died hard. What's the note say? Can't make out the words for blood.'

'I've figured it out. It says that Wolf Taker is on his way to Los Conchos to sell Mandy to the slave-traders there.' Jordan's mouth was pulled tight, his lips white around the edges as he set his gaze on Loomis. 'A white woman brings big money down there, especially a blonde one. If she's taken all the way to Mexico City, the price'll double, maybe treble.'

Loomis spat. 'Goddamn slavers! That's one thing I'll never have to answer for when I go to Glory.'

Jordan couldn't help but smile faintly. It sounded strange to hear a man of Loomis's low morals get so indignant, but even Matt Loomis had his scruples, it seemed, and white slavery was the bottom of the barrel as far as he was concerned.

Then Loomis suddenly snapped his head up. 'Judas! Who did this, Chris? Who cut up that Injun and then left the note?'

Jordan glanced up and nodded towards the top of the ridge. Loomis tensed as he saw a rider sitting a grey horse up there, but only for a moment. Then the man wheeled his mount and dropped out of sight over the crest.

'The hell is he?'

Jordan shook his head. 'I'd say he's the one who nailed Shawn the other night.'

'You going after him?'

'No. By the time I unhitched my horse and saddled-up he'll be long gone.'

'What's he playin at? I mean, shooting Shawn that way, now — this? Why would he help us?'

'He's helping me — and I don't have an answer, Matt. But let's get saddled-up and ride.'

Loomis didn't move. 'To Los Conchos?'

'Where else?'

'Chris, if there's a corner of hell on earth, it's Los Conchos. We'll never get out alive. Unless they decide they want us that way so they can sell *us* too!'

'That's the chance we take.'

'*You* take: not me.'

'Not this again, Matt! Damnit, I . . .' Jordan was turning as he spoke and he stopped now, covered by Loomis's cocked rifle.

'No, this is the end of the trail for me, Chris. I savvy how you want to get that gal back, but my only interest is the strongbox. You tell me where it is and I'll start back for the border.' He jerked his head towards the ridge. 'You won't be alone — your ghost rider'll be there to help out when you need him.'

Suddenly Loomis staggered as Jordan swung his own rifle, and the barrels clashed together as it struck Loomis's Winchester from his grasp. Then Jordan kicked the other's legs out from under him and, as Loomis sprawled, jammed his rifle barrel under the man's jaw, towering above him.

'I need you along, Matt. You've been there before . . . I need you to show me the way and to get me into the town.'

Loomis lay there, breathing hard, looking up into those deadly eyes. He swore softly. 'You sure must have one helluva shine for this woman of yours.'

He was surprised to see Jordan's eyes suddenly soften, and the man's voice held the suggestion of a tremor as he

'She's like the beat of my heart, . . .'

Loomis's frown deepened. He was oddly touched by Jordan's answer.

'You come with me, Matt, or you'll never get your hands on that strongbox,' Jordan told him. 'I swear it.'

Loomis thought of several arguments but suddenly shrugged his shoulders. 'OK, OK. Hell, the day I made this deal with you I must've been outa my head!'

Jordan lowered the rifle and extended his left hand to help Loomis to his feet. For a moment they stood face to face, eyes only inches apart.

'Thanks, Matt.'

Loomis scowled. 'There'll be a settlin' after I get that payroll, don't think there won't.'

Jordan nodded, knowing the man spoke the truth. No matter what Loomis agreed to now, he would never forget that Jordan had roughed him up and got the upper hand several times.

Matt Loomis wasn't the kind of *hombre* who could live with that.

Matt Loomis wasn't familiar with the country around the sierra and they travelled by night to get through the rugged ranges. Once they saw campfires on a rise above them and several men moving about between the fires and where they led their mounts silently by below.

'*Federales?*' asked Loomis quietly.

'Most likely,' Jordan allowed, and they turned down-slope away from the fires. He swore softly to himself. Salazar wouldn't give up now that he knew Jordan was in Mexico. And the officer must have recognized Loomis as the man who had put out his eye years earlier.

No, there would be a manhunt now and Salazar would likely make for some town where he could send a telegraph message ahead for other *federales* to watch for the *gringos*.

It was a hassle Jordan could do without but it was there and all they uld do now was try to stay out of sight until they caught up with Wolf Taker.

The bloodstained note hadn't said if the Apache had any men with him but it was likely he would have a few. Jordan's guts knotted at the thought that Mandy might be shared out among them.

He quickly pushed the images from his mind but his palms were sweating. He had made himself a promise, too: if he was caught by Wolf Taker or looked like being taken, then he aimed to kill Mandy, save her the degradation and humiliation and agony of a life of slavery. Once he had seen a white woman who had somehow managed to escape Mexican slavers and the sight was something he would never forget.

She had been out of her mind, had been terribly abused physically, and . . .

'*Goddamnittohell*!' he snapped suddenly, startling Loomis.

'Hell, man, you scared me white! What's up?'

'Nothing. Didn't mean to speak aloud.'

Loomis was quiet a spell and then said softly, 'Best not think about her, Chris. It'll drive you loco.'

Jordan nodded slowly, thinking he was already loco with anguish over Mandy.

But he wouldn't swerve from the trail. He would do whatever it took to either rescue Mandy or put her out of her misery.

★　★　★

By daylight they were through the sierras and facing a broken country that pulsed with heat even before the sun had been in the sky for an hour. The land was harsh but there were patches of colour from sparse vegetation. Pipestem cactus and candelabras, the yellow fruit and purple flowers of the cholla plant, agaves, maguey, yucca, and in a line of low hills where water of some kind was indicated, the green of Peruvian peppertrees amongst creosote and mesquite.

'Salazar'll have to come this way for water,' Loomis pointed out. 'Be best if we avoid that hogback and pick the next.'

'You're in charge from here on in, Matt,' Jordan agreed, although he knew both canteens were less than half-full.

'We're gonna be mighty thirsty by the time we sight Los Conchos, but it'll be better if we don't leave tracks.'

'I did a stint in the army. They let us go thirsty and hungry just before we made an attack. It only served to make us fight harder, because we knew there'd be food and water afterwards.'

Loomis grunted. 'Sounds like the kinda thing the army'd do. All right. Let's move and get into some shade before the heat of the day.'

They rested in a fold of the hills and before they started again a funnelling dust cloud way out told them that Salazar was heading for the water-course.

While Loomis dozed, Jordan scouted around and climbed out of the fold, made his way from rock to rock to the other slope above the trees and the watercourse. He saw it was a streambed but it wasn't flowing, only a series of shallow, muddy pools. Three of them. And there were dead animals in each one.

'Wolf Taker!' he breathed. The man had fouled the waterholes to discourage pursuit.

He scouted around, keeping an eye on the approaching soldiers and just before it was time to get out so he wouldn't be discovered, he found a trace of the Apache band.

He dropped prone, face against the ground, looking carefully from every angle. Once he had used the light to pick up the shallow depressions of unshod hoofs that had been only partially brushed-out with a leafy branch, he had a direction.

He was excited when he got back to where Loomis was snoring softly, nudged the man awake and told him to mount-up.

'We're going after Wolf Taker! I've found his trail!'

It was an exaggeration but at least it was a start and by sundown he had picked up faint signs in several other places, confirming the direction the Apache was taking. He also had worked out there were five riders, likely four men and a woman. The lighter impression of one horse's hoofs indicated this.

It had to be Mandy and he found his heart hammering at the thought that he was actually closing in, for the trail was only hours old now.

He didn't want to stop searching but Loomis said Los Conchos wasn't far now and it was likely that Wolf Taker was already in the town, making a deal with the slavers.

Jordan felt as if his insides had suddenly fallen out at the gun-runner's words.

'But if he's smart,' Loomis added, bringing Jordan's head up with a snap, 'he'll leave her outside of town, hid with the others, go in and bring the slaver out to look her over.'

'Why would he do that?'

'Hell, a lone Injun in a place like Los Conchos, trying to sell off a white woman with golden hair? They'd slit his throat and take her off him before you could spit. Taking the slaver out to the camp is the safest. And Wolf Taker's done this before, I'd say.'

Jordan nodded slowly. 'Then we find the camp while he's in town talking the slaver into coming out with him into the hills . . . '

Loomis ran a hand around his stubbled jaw. 'It's one way.'

'You know another?'

'We wait beside the Los Conchos trail and jump the slaver on his return journey. He'll have your wife with him and he'll be alone. It'll save trying to locate the Injuns' camp.'

'We hit their camp, Matt!' Jordan said faintly. 'I want Wolf Taker.'

Loomis sighed. 'Figured you'd say that. Well, you're the tracker. You'll have to find the place — but we'll be up agin at least three of them — five if Wolf's returned with the slaver. Who might also bring along a man to side him . . . '

'Let's go, Matt. I'm too close to pussyfoot around any longer.'

'Yeah, I know.' Loomis actually sounded sympathetic. Jordan and Loomis crossed the low ridge ahead and angled down the far face in their search for Wolf Taker's camp.

In the distance, on the slopes of a far mountain, they saw the sprawling white and brown dots of Los Conchos. It was a good position for a lawless town, giving commanding views of approaches on three sides. The fourth was a steep slope above the town, difficult if not impossible for horses to traverse without sending scree slides down into the village itself, giving warning.

Sitting their weary mounts in the shade of some trees on a rise, Loomis studied the countryside between their position and the mountain village. He lifted an arm and pointed towards a harsh landscape, full of misleading shadows.

'There. That'd be the best place for Wolf to set up a temporary hideout.'

Jordan could see nothing at first, then made out an overhang of rock and, beneath it, what he had thought was bare ground, he was able to make out now as the walls of a wind-scoured basin.

'How big is it?'

'Twenty or thirty yards across, but the sides are cut deep by gullies from water erosion in flood times. Plenty places to hide a small bunch of men and hosses.'

'Let's go take a look.'

They dismounted and moved towards the overhang on foot. The ground was broken and both slipped and sprawled several times. But they took more care when they were closer and when they saw it was safe to go right under the overhang itself, Loomis took the lead and worked his way anti-clockwise around the rim of the basin.

Jordan held his rifle at the ready, breath hissing through his teeth, heart rate accelerating. Then suddenly Loomis dropped flat and Jordan crouched on his hams. Matt Loomis glanced over his shoulder, used his eyebrows and an inclination of his head to indicate something was below and slightly left.

As they started to move forward, Jordan heard a man's voice.

'Ah, you speak the truth, Señor Wolf! She is a beauty one, eh? Stand her up and let me see all of her.'

Loomis looked sharply at Jordan and swore when he saw it was too late to stop the man. Jordan pushed past, moving quietly but swiftly over the harsh ground. He came to a sun-baked chest-high ridge of clay and looked over and down.

In the deep gully beyond were four Apaches — one of them was Wolf Taker — two Mexicans, and Mandy.

He had only time to note she was dishevelled, her hair tangled, her clothes torn and filthy. He was in time to see Wolf Taker wrench the dress from her shoulders, revealing her nakedness beneath. The breath of one of the Mexicans hissed in audibly and the man stepped forward, reaching for one of Mandy's exposed breasts, thumb and forefinger ready to pinch pink flesh . . .

Jordan shot the man through the head, saw blood splash across Mandy's white flesh, an instant before he swung the rifle to the other Mexican and shot him in the stomach. The Indians scattered and by then Loomis was shooting, too. He brought down one man who had taken only two steps, the bullet snapping his spine. Another swung up a rifle at Loomis who punched two bullets into his chest, the man twisting as he fell.

Jordan downed one of the two remaining Indians and the last one was Wolf Taker who ran at the screaming woman, a naked blade slashing at her body. She fell and the knife missed and Wolf Taker stumbled.

Jordan let out a roar, came slipping and sliding down into the gully and as the Apache started up, kicked him savagely in the face. Wolf sprawled across Mandy's legs, darted a look of wild hatred at Jordan and flung himself on top of Mandy, hands clawing for her throat.

Jordan kicked the man in the spine, leaned down, twisted his fingers in the lank hair. Wolf refused to release his hold, hissed and growled as his hair started to pull out of his scalp but tightened his grip on the woman's slim throat. Jordan gouged his eyes and still the Apache refused to let go. Panting, wild, frantic now, Jordan drew his sixgun, rammed the barrel against the Indian's temple and fired, three times, pushing the gory corpse to one side. He dropped the smoking gun and knelt swiftly, prising at the fingers still clamped around his wife's neck.

The Apache death grip wouldn't give and Jordan gritted his teeth, broke the fingers one by one until he heard

Mandy give a strangled gasp and chest heaved as air finally reached ____ bursting lungs.

She coughed and retched and he clasped her to him as she fought to suck down more and more life-giving air.

Loomis stood above him, draped the torn and filthy dress over the woman's naked back and buttocks, looked around at the dead men. One of the Mexicans was still alive, crying to Mother Mary to help him and to forgive him for his sins.

Loomis sent him to ask forgiveness from his God in person.

By then Mandy had settled down some, and she clung to Jordan, her bruised and battered body shaken by terrible sobs.

'We oughtn't to stick around here,' Loomis said worriedly. 'That shooting might bring someone from Los Conchos, or even Salazar.'

Jordan nodded, stroking Mandy's knotted hair. 'A moment, Matt. Just give her a moment.'

Loomis smothered a curse. 'I'll bring the horses.'

Jordan had a spare dress for Mandy in one of his saddle-bags, as well as underclothes. He had brought them because he figured she would need them — and hoped clean and familiar clothing might help ease the pain of her shock after her ordeal. He'd heard such things worked with distraught women.

It was the mark of a thoughtful and caring man and Mandy kissed him gently before dressing behind a rock. Then Loomis, on the rim called, '*Federales!* Must've heard the gunfire! They're coming in fast!'

10

Grey Rider

Colonel Salazar had been too eager.

He had refused to rest his men on the long chase through the sierras to the sun-blasted country just this side of Los Conchos.

He had found the dead Indians and slavers in the shallow basin, watched helplessly as the three fugitives fled over the hills, heading north. They had taken time to scatter the dead men's horses first, although it seemed that the woman had taken a claybank that had belonged to one of the Mexicans from Los Conchos.

After his men had rounded up the scattered horses, Salazar chose the remaining slaver's horse, a big chestnut, for himself, then picked his strongest men for the rest. In all he now had six men mounted on reasonably fresh horses. The rest of the troop, some wounded from the fight back at the *rancheria*, could drag along behind. He would lead the others on the chase and with a little luck and lot of curses and slashing with his quirt, would overtake Jordan before sundown.

But Salazar was too optimistic. Sundown came and the fugitives weren't even in sight when the near-exhausted *federales* drove their weary mounts on to the crest of the ridge where the colonel was fruitlessly sweeping the countryside ahead with his field glasses.

'They are well hidden — or riding faster than I thought!' he cursed briefly. 'We can do nothing but make camp for the night.'

And it was a cheerless camp, lacking both food and water.

★   ★   ★

Jordan knew they could not hope to keep up the pace they had set since leaving the basin.

The horses were feeling the strain, not only from the rugged, undulating country, but also the flints that were scattered in their thousands underfoot. Twice he had prised sharp-edged flints from under the buckskin's shoes, noting how worn and cracked the metal had become. He figured they would be lucky to make the Rio without the horse throwing a shoe.

Loomis scouted ahead, climbing some rocks, while Jordan wiped down the sweating mounts as well as he could with the ragged remains of the frock Mandy had been wearing at the time of her rescue. She sat silently now, in between two rocks, knees drawn up, arms wrapped about her legs. She had a glazed look, her face swollen, bruised and cut.

Jordan felt his heart go out to her, trying to imagine the hell she must have gone through at Wolf Taker's ds. He was worried about how it was going to affect her.

Until now, she hadn't had time to think about anything but escape, but this enforced rest was going to allow her to remember her ordeal in detail — perhaps too much detail. She shivered even as he looked and he saw twin tears tracking through the filth on her cheeks.

'Chris?'

He crossed to kneel beside her quickly. 'I'm here Mandy . . . it's all right now.'

Her haunted eyes searched his face in the fast-fading light. Suddenly, one of her dirty, broken-nailed hands gripped his arm tightly enough to make him wince.

'I'm — I'm too — soiled to go back to being your wife,' she whispered, face twisting with self-abhorrence. 'The . . . things they did . . . '

He pulled her against his chest awkwardly, stroking the knotted, befouled golden hair. 'No one'll ever

do anything like that to you a
Mandy, I swear it.'

She pushed back and anger flashed
across her misshapen face. 'They've
already *done* it, don't you understand?
I'm already defiled, contaminated!'

'Mandy, stop this!' he snapped,
grabbing her by the shoulders, hearing
the hysteria rising in her. His fingers
dug into her flesh, deliberately brutal.
His eyes bored deeply into hers. 'You
had no control over what happened.
The men who did it to you are dead
— you saw me kill them. Now get hold
of yourself.'

She fixed him with a cold look. 'You
took so damn *long* to come . . . So
. . . long!'

'I know. I'm sorry. But I'm here now
and you're safe. See? Feel my arms
about you? Hear my heartbeat against
your face? You're *here*, where you
belong.'

She broke then, the sobs racking her
as she clung to him, her tears soaking
through his shirt. He figured she

would be better once she had cried it out . . .

* * *

Although Mandy slept deeply, she was still very jumpy the next morning, snapping at Loomis because he had not yet found enough water to wash in properly.

Jordan tried to calm her down, figuring there would likely be other incidents like this before she finally came to terms with what had happened to her. He deliberately broke camp early and was dozing in the saddle around mid-morning when Loomis suddenly shouted, jerking him awake. The man was pointing off to the left and Jordan slewed quickly in the saddle and blinked to get the last of the sleep from his eyes.

Mandy was riding off into the wilderness, lashing at the slaver's claybank she rode with her rein ends.

Jordan immediately spurred after her, hearing the buckskin's grunt of protest, swearing under his breath at having to put his weary mount through this extra strain.

Mandy didn't look behind, lashed her mount up a rise and crossed the crest in a cloud of dust. Jordan swore again and went after her, raking with his spurs. Loomis hadn't joined in the pursuit, was sitting his dun calmly enough, hands folded on the saddlehorn.

Over the ridge, Jordan saw the girl far down the slope, going too fast for its steepness. He called her name hoarsely as her mount went down in a flurry of dust and gravel. Mandy sailed over its head, struck the slope on her shoulders, slipping and rolling and spinning.

He slid the buckskin down, throwing his weight back on to its haunches, leapt from the saddle and staggered and stumbled into the cloud of rolling dust. He found Mandy curled around a bush, semi-conscious, scratched and grazed, but apparently otherwise unhurt.

The horse had righted itself but was

limping badly and Jordan tightened his lips when he saw that the right foreleg was broken.

He drew his sixgun, rammed the muzzle into one of the horse's ears and dropped hammer. The shot was muffled but still slapped through the hills.

'What the hell did you think you were doing?' he asked the girl tersely, as Loomis topped the crest and put the dun cautiously down the slope.

'I-I don't know, Chris! I-I just felt this terrible wave of panic and I had to *run*!' She covered her face with her hands. 'I'm sorry. I didn't mean to . . . ' She gestured helplessly towards the horse Jordan had had to shoot.

'Mean to or not,' snapped Loomis, as he skidded to a halt. 'You've slowed us way down now! You'll have to ride double with Jordan.'

He looked steadily at the other man and Jordan said quietly, 'She couldn't help it, Matt. No use standing here jawing about it.'

Loomis's face was tight, his eyes

narrowed as he watched Jordan help the shaken girl up into his saddle and then swing up behind her.

'She's your responsibility, Chris. If Salazar shows I ain't about to wait around while you hobble along behind, I'm heading lickety-split for the border.'

Jordan nodded. 'Fair enough, Matt — '

He broke off as Loomis's sixgun suddenly covered him. 'Just one thing — where's the strong-box? I figure you owe me that much, Chris.'

'Guess I do at that,' Jordan said slowly, watching the Colt. 'OK. You've done your share, Matt. Know the Pipestems?'

Loomis's face sharpened. 'You mean them queer rock formations like chimneys standing up in the hills west of Presidio?'

'That's them. Line up the middle one with Mount Brewster and halfway along the line you see a wall of coloured clay. Several layers, red, yellow, blue-grey. Colours end against a cutbank, or what was a cutbank till I collapsed it over the strongbox. It'll take a deal of digging, Matt.'

Loomis squinted at him. 'The hell were you doing so far south?'

'Following Waco. He was the one had the strongbox and he kept trying to lose me. Then I eventually rode into his ambush.'

Loomis seemed to think about this. 'Then dumped his body a long ways from where you'd buried the box . . . ' He nodded to himself, as if accepting Jordan's word. '*Adios*, Chris.' He touched the brim of his hat to Mandy. 'Hope you both make it — but don't bother looking me up again, Chris, we're through, you and me.'

Jordan snapped him a brief salute as the man wheeled his dun and put it once more up the slope. He found the girl watching him intently and he forced a smile.

'Don't worry, Mandy, we'll make it all right.'

He wished he felt as confident as he tried to sound.

⋆　⋆　⋆

Salazar's men fell so far behind he grew tired of looking for them. He bared his teeth and raked his horse's already bloody flanks with his guthook spurs.

Topping a rise, he glimpsed a single rider going up the slope of a distant ridge. He groped in his saddle-bags for his field glasses, focused quickly before the man disappeared over the crest. It wasn't Jordan, but it could be Loomis . . .

His teeth ground together as the man dropped from sight to the far side of the ridge. He swept the glasses downwards and from side to side, searching amongst the sparse vegetation — and finally found what he was looking for: a horse, staggering under the weight of two people; a big man and a woman with lank, once-golden hair.

'Ah!' he said with great satisfaction as

he focused better on his target. 'The Aztec gods of my ancestors have not forsaken me! Oh, no, *gringo*, they have sent me the bounty I have longed for.'

He unshipped the long-barrelled Mauser rifle, checked the clip magazine and found there were four cartridges remaining. He worked one into the breech and, holding the awkward weapon out to one side, spurred his mount down the slope, uncaring now whether Jordan saw him. For he knew, weary though the big chestnut was, he could easily overtake Jordan's buckskin with its double load.

He glanced behind but his men weren't in sight yet. No matter. He wouldn't need them. It would give him great pleasure to handle this alone.

★ ★ ★

For one blazing moment Jordan couldn't believe his eyes when he saw Salazar sitting his horse on the trail ahead. The man's rifle was pointed directly at Mandy and his arm tightened instinctively about her slim waist.

'I think you have reached what you *gringos* call the 'trail's end', Jor-dan! You and your *señora*!'

The colonel bowed slightly in Mandy's direction as she sat there, dull-eyed, not yet truly comprehending the situation. Jordan slowly lifted his hands shoulder-high and, as he did so, spoke quietly, his mouth close to her ear.

'When I say so, go sideways out of the saddle — to your left.'

Still sounding a little dazed, she half-turned her head and asked, 'What . . . ?'

'What're you talking about?' demanded Salazar.

'Just telling her to stay calm, Colonel. She's mighty jumpy after what she's been through.'

The Mexican's teeth flashed. 'Of course, but not *too* calm, *señora*! I like my women with some fight in them!'

She frowned, turning towards Jordan

again and he saw it rising behind her eyes, the realization that this man with the rifle was going to subject her to the same abuse she had suffered at the hands of the Apaches, maybe worse. Her mouth opened in a scream, exploding into the hot afternoon, hammering at his eardrums, startling Salazar as he had hoped it would.

'Drop!' he snapped, thrusting her to the left and she screamed again as she began to fall.

Jordan's sixgun came blurring up from its holster and he fired at the same instant that Salazar's rifle crashed. Jordan twisted violently in the saddle and rolled back over the horse's rump, spilling awkwardly to the ground.

At the same time, Salazar reared up straight in his stirrups, his mouth slack, his single eye glittering, mouth working. Then blood spilled over his bottom lip and he sagged to the right, instinctively still trying to work the bolt of his rifle. Dazed, the world a blur behind a sheet of blazing yellow light, Jordan triggered two more shots before the Colt leapt from his weakened grip as he plunged into darkness.

Salazar's body jerked with the strike of the lead and he sagged on to his face, the big chestnut stomping him as it reared and bucked in fright at the nearness of the gunfire. Then it ran off and stopped several yards away, snorting and pawing the ground.

The girl sat up, bruised and a little dazed. Brushing hair out of her eyes, she looked from the dead Mexican officer to where Jordan lay, still and bloody. She rubbed at her temples, trying to ease the pain in her head, cried his name and crawled swiftly to him.

Salazar's bullet had taken him through the lower right side, passing between the ribs without touching them, but it had torn the flesh badly and there was a lot of blood. She was weeping now and her hands were shaking, and for precious seconds she froze, unable to think.

Then at last she stirred herself and in

seconds had torn off the lower part of her dress and made a pad and a crude bandage. By the time she had tied it in place, Jordan was coming round, his face grey with shock and pain. He looked past the girl's shoulder to where Salazar lay.

'We have to get out of here. Lend a hand, Mandy.' One hand pressed against his wounded side, he struggled to his feet as she got her shoulder under his left arm and slowly stood upright. 'Get me to my horse and then see if you can catch Salazar's mount. We'll be able to move faster if we don't have to ride double.'

It took time but she eventually caught the abused chestnut, spoke soothingly to it while stroking its sweat-slick chest, calming it down. She led it across to where Jordan stood leaning against the buckskin and she helped him into the saddle. While he reloaded his sixgun she mounted and they started off, side by side — just as the first of the *federales* appeared on the ridge above.

Rifles crashed and bullets kicked dust in half-a-dozen places, two even thudding into Salazar's body. They urged their protesting horses on and up the opposite slope even as the Mexicans realized their commander was dead. Rage surged through the *federales* then and, led by Salazar's loyal sergeant, they charged recklessly down into the hollow.

Jordan didn't waste time or lead shooting at them. The girl drew ahead, kept stopping and waiting for him to catch up. He waved her on angrily, but she was reluctant to leave him. Maybe his wounding hadn't been such a bad thing after all, Jordan thought: at least while she was worrying about him she didn't have time to think about her own past ordeal.

But she was not in any condition for a long dangerous chase: nor was he for that matter; the rude bandage was already soaked with fresh blood. But they didn't have any choice and all they could do was to keep on going, urged on by the Mexicans' bullets.

But they reached the crest and the soldiers now down in the hollow, dismounted and took steadier aim, loosing off a rattling volley. Jordan ducked as lead buzzed overhead but the girl was already across and below the crest. She glanced back at him, white-faced, and he waved her on wearily.

The slope was steep and required both hands to manage the weakened mounts. The only safe way was to zigzag although it was slower and made them easier targets, but Jordan knew that neither of them would make it going straight down in a steep slide. Before they were halfway down, the soldiers reached the top and started shooting again. The bullets were closer now, kicking into the slope near the horses' hoofs, clipping dry twigs from the sparse trees they weaved between.

Then a rifle crashed from below and in front, off to one side. Jordan looked back in time to see the sergeant's body rolling lifelessly down the slope. A soldier dropped his rifle and clawed at a shoulder. Two more soldiers crashed to the ground, writhing. The remaining two retreated over the ridge and Jordan hauled rein, calling to Mandy to keep riding. But she, too, halted her panting horse and looked at the rider on a grey horse who had appeared out of an arroyo. He lifted a hand in mocking salute before turning his mount and disappearing into the brush.

'Who the hell *is* that *hombre*?' Jordan asked aloud: he had been expecting their rescuer to be Matt Loomis. Instead it had been the mysterious grey rider who had saved his neck a couple of times already.

Mandy said it wasn't anyone she knew but he had a feeling she wasn't too sure about that. Still, this was no time for a discussion about it.

'Let's get moving,' he said, gasping a little with the pain in his side. 'With luck, we'll have a straight run to the border now.'

They reached the Rio after dark, the

moon rising early and spilling a wedge of silver across the shallow water. They stripped off their filthy clothes, rinsed them as clean as possible, and then plunged in to wash themselves.

The tepid river water felt good against Jordan's wound and he frowned as he watched Mandy scrub herself over and over with handfuls of coarse river sand, rubbing until, finally, in places the outer skin began to peel away.

He grabbed her hand as she scooped up more sand and prepared to start scrubbing once more. She looked at him angrily, tried to pull her hand away.

'That's enough, Mandy,' he told her quietly but firmly. 'You're scraping yourself raw.'

'I still feel dirty!' she hissed, eyes blazing.

'I know, my love,' he told her gently. 'It's a feeling that likely won't go away for a spell yet. But wait until we can get some lye soap and hot water. Once you have a proper bath and get into clean, decent clothes, you'll feel better. I promise you.'

Then she began to sob and fell into his waiting arms . . .

★　★　★

They slept amongst the brush on the American side of the river and Jordan was awake at first light.

His side was stiff and sore to touch and he felt feverish, his mouth on fire and his mind as if one step removed from reality. Mandy stirred when she heard him up and about. When she saw the way he was favouring his side, she rose quickly and insisted on examining the wound.

'It looks a little infected. I'll boil some water and bathe it. You should see a doctor. Is there a town close by?'

He shrugged. 'Guess Presidio'd be nearest.'

'Good. We'll go there.'

'I'll be all right.'

'Yes. After a doctor sees to your

wound, you will. So we go to Presidio.'

She sounded firm and he had to admit he wouldn't mind if a sawbones did take a look at the wound. They were on the trail in half an hour.

Crossing a stretch of treeless flats near the foothills of a low range, Jordan suddenly halted, holding up a hand swiftly as the girl went to speak.

'Sure I heard gunfire. A long way off, but I'm certain that's what it was.'

'It's nothing to do with us, Chris,' she said sharply. 'The sooner you see a doctor the better . . . '

She broke off as he pointed over her shoulder. Frowning, she turned and saw, poking up behind the low saw-tooths, three chimney-like rocks reaching a couple of hundred feet into the air.

'The Pipestems?' she asked tautly, and he nodded.

'That's where I figure the gunfire came from. Matt's out there somewhere . . . '

'He didn't even come back to help

224

when Salazar attacked us! He *must* have heard the shooting!'

She saw arguing with him was a waste of time. He was already turning in the direction of the Pipestems. She sighed resignedly and put the big chestnut after the buckskin.

They arrived in just over an hour and Jordan went in on foot, rifle in hand, looking past the earthen wall with its stripes of coloured clay. Someone had dug deep into the cutbank, leaving an empty gaping hole, the short-handled pick and shovel he and Loomis had brought lying on the ground.

Beside them lay Loomis's hat, muddy and trampled, a bullet hole showing in the crown.

As Jordan stood on a pile of earth, the girl somewhere behind him, a man appeared behind a breastwork of eroded soil. It was Matt Loomis and he had a bloodstained bandanna tied around his head. His shirt had been used to make a second bandage around his upper chest. He was greyfaced, his legs weak. They gave way under him abruptly so that he tumbled down the slope to sprawl near the hole in the cutbank soil. Jordan stumbled forward, kneeling beside the wounded gun-runner.

'Matt, what the hell happened?'

'*I* happened to him, Jordan, or should I call you 'Frank Christian' like I used to back in Diamondback Creek?'

Jordan instinctively reached for the rifle he had laid on the ground, but the newcomer's gun roared and a bullet kicked Jordan's Winchester out of reach.

Still crouched, he stared up at the man straddling the grey horse but it was Mandy who spoke.

'I thought you looked vaguely familiar back there after you drove off the Mexicans but I thought I must be mistaken. You're a long way from home, Sheriff Plumm.'

'Just plain 'Andy Plumm' these days, ma'am,' the man said looking lean and mean, watching Jordan closely. 'Your fault, Jordan.'

Jordan arched his eyebrows. 'Now

how could that be?'

' 'Cause I never recognized you for an outlaw when you came to my town. I went to a lot of trouble to find out who you really were after you gunned-down them two *hombres* . . . I reckoned that'd get me in good with Miles Prendergast, who really ran that town, as you know.' His mouth tightened as he shook his head. 'But it didn't. Son of a bitch fired me for not doin' my job proper. Kicked me out without a pension or nothin' . . .

Jordan glanced at Mandy. Her face was stiff as she listened to Plumm talking about her father: although he had 'kicked her out', too, just like Plumm, she had never stopped caring for him but she knew him to be a hard, stubborn man.

'How come you been turning up and saving my neck a couple of times, Andy?' Jordan asked.

Plumm spat. 'When I found out who you were, I heard about that strongbox you was s'posed to've buried with the payroll still in it — ten thousand bucks.'

He was watching both Jordan and Loomis clearly now, gripping his rifle tightly.

'Knew Loomis'd be involved and I found out he'd gone off with you to look for Mandy there. I'd just missed you at that tradin' post: damned Injun got there ahead of me — ' Again Plumm spat. 'Anyways, I knew Loomis wouldn't be workin' for nothin' and I got to one of his men, found out he had some kinda deal with you — a fifty-fifty split of somethin' was all he knew. So I figured all I had to do was keep you alive till you found your missus and then you and Loomis'd head for the strongbox for the pay-off.'

'And you aimed to buy in,' Jordan finished.

Plumm shrugged. 'Seemed fair to me. After I shot those Mexes and realized Loomis wasn't with you, I figured you must've told him where to find the box and tracked him to here.'

Jordan looked down at Loomis. 'He take it all?'

Loomis rolled his pain-filled eyes to Jordan's face and Plumm said tightly, 'Go ahead! Tell him!'

'There was no money in the box, Chris,' Loomis said.

'What?' Jordan felt as if he had been punched in the belly.

'Full of old ledgers and papers and letters . . . found one that told the story. It was a decoy, Chris. You recollect how we all wondered why they handed over the strongbox so easy, didn't put up much of a fight? How we thought it queer that no express company agents came searching for us like they usually do when one of their payroll trains is held-up? They sent the money by stage-coach! In a leather satchel in the goddamn luggage boot!'

Jordan stared at the wounded man, remembered Plumm, and snapped his head around quickly, just in time to see the man lifting his rifle.

'I don't have no use for you two now,' Plumm said, 'but I reckon even old Skinflint Prendergast ought to pay a reward to the man who brings his daughter back safe from bein' took by Apaches . . . '

'I'll tell how you killed Matt and Chris!' Mandy said quickly, as Plumm's finger tightened on the trigger.

He sneered. 'Won't matter none. They're outlaws, Miles'll still pay ransom to have you back in one piece, I reckon. He might pretend he don't care, but I know that old son of a bitch and way down he'd do anythin' to have you back with him . . . '

He swung the rifle towards Loomis and Jordan rolled backwards, grasping his Colt and firing through the open bottom of the holster. The bullet grazed the neck of the grey horse and it reared as Plumm fired and his shot thudded into the ground beside Loomis.

Jordan rolled again, feeling the wrenching tear of flesh in his side, Colt clear of leather. He slewed his long body around as Plumm let out a roar and jumped the big grey forward, rifle blazing. Jordan slid down off the mound of earth, hearing Mandy call his name, and then he spun on to his back, emptying the gun up at the raging ex-lawman.

Plumm's riddled body shuddered and hurtled from the saddle, head-first, flopped face down and was still.

When the gunsmoke cleared, Mandy rushed to adjust the bandage on Jordan's wound to staunch the flow of fresh blood. Loomis lay there in his own agony, the girl moving across to help him.

'All for nothing, Chris,' Loomis said quietly. 'All for nothing . . . '

Jordan said, 'For you. But I got Mandy back. That counts for everything for me.'

She smiled at him warmly as she looked at the wound in Loomis's chest and told him he would live once a doctor took out the bullet that was still lodged in the muscle.

'Well, guess I came out with something after all — my life.' He sobered, fixing Jordan with a straight stare. 'I owe you, Chris. Plumm was gonna kill me for sure. Say! I got a deal of money waiting for me back in Rockwall, s'pose I give you two love-birds a wedding present? Kinda late, I know, but how's a couple of thousand sound? Just to get you started.'

'Sounds mighty damn good to me,' Jordan allowed.

'Aw, come on Mandy! Don't do that! Chris, will you call off this wife of yours? I ain't used to being kissed by nice ladies . . . '

Jordan winked at Mandy. 'She'll come back to me when she's ready.'

Mandy smiled, stood up and walked across to slip an arm around Jordan's shoulders.

'And that's any time — any time at all!'

Loomis groaned and looked away as they kissed.